PETER
PUMPKIN
GOES
TRICK
-or-
TREATING

PETER PUMPKIN GOES TRICK -or- TREATING

Peter Nanra

ARCHWAY
PUBLISHING

Archway Publishing books may be ordered through booksellers or by contacting:

Archway Publishing
1663 Liberty Drive
Bloomington, IN 47403
www.archwaypublishing.com
1 (888) 242-5904

ISBN: 978-1-4808-1913-9 (sc)
ISBN: 978-1-4808-1914-6 (hc)
ISBN: 978-1-4808-1915-3 (e)

Library of Congress Control Number: 2015943740

Print information available on the last page.

Archway Publishing rev. date: 7/1/2015

CHAPTER 1
HELLO

It was not the noises and shrieks of the witches, ghosts, were-wolves, and other ghouls on this night that were keeping me awake. Rather, it was the sheer excitement of going trick-or-treating for the very first time. It was two days before Halloween.

We knew the ghouls would be out late at this time of year. Not only were they out having their usual fun, but they were also showing off their Halloween costumes to one another—witches dressed up as werewolves, ghosts as vampires, goblins as bats, and so on. Isn't that strange, though? Why does a witch even need to dress up on Halloween? Witches are scary enough; they don't need to dress up as another creature. No ghoul needs a costume for Halloween. Ghouls are creatures that for hundreds of years have tormented, scared, and, generally speaking, given us pumpkins a difficult time. They stay in hiding during the day and then make an appearance at night. Two days before Halloween, they feel this is their time to shine.

Like I said, however, those noises didn't bother me in the least. I wasn't scared. This was the best time of year. Two more days and two more nights of sleep, and my friends and I would go trick-or-treating. The phrase is weird, though. I mean, are we asking for a treat or a trick? No one wants a trick, and no one wants to perform a trick—not me anyway. I want a treat. Besides, no one actually ever performs a trick for a trick-or-treater. But I'm not sure about that because, like I said, this was the first time I was going out.

This was very exciting. We would go out to the city, knock on people's doors, and they would give us candy. This happens only one day out of the year. We would get all types of candy—chocolate, juju fruit and chewy candy, gum, potato chips, and lollipops. I love all types of chocolate: milk chocolate, dark chocolate, with or without nuts. Chocolate mixed in with peanut butter is one of my favorites. Peanut butter cups are like that. Do Crispy Crunch bars have peanut butter? I can't remember. Last Halloween, my friends and I ate so much chocolate that we developed pimples the size of M&M's on our skin. Needless to say, none of the elders were pleased with us.

On Halloween, people give out so much candy that it takes us months to finish it all. The mounds of candy that accumulate in the Patch are phenomenal. So much candy gets collected that it can take months before Halloween for us to plan how to store it all.

The process of storing the candy is quite complicated. After collection, it gets brought back to the Patch, where it gets registered, examined, separated, and sorted. Kit Kat bars go in the Kit Kat pile. Mars bars go in the Mars bar pile. There are different types of gum that go in different piles. Bubble gum goes in its own pile, further sorted by flavor. Gum designed to make your breath feel fresh goes in another pile. Well, you get the idea. Like I said, it's a very complicated process.

I must say that I have become impressed with the efficiency, neatness, and organization of the whole endeavor. A storage spot has to be voted on and approved. Last year, a large hole was dug right underneath the kitchen. Schedules for the trick-or-treaters' departure and arrival times had to be made. For us pumpkins, trick-or-treating isn't just about collecting candy; it's about everyone getting together, united for a single cause. We become unified as a species because we're all striving to achieve a common goal in a tradition that dates back hundreds of years.

It's very difficult to describe in words the amount of energy and time we spend preparing for Halloween. The tiniest detail is accounted for. Every pumpkin has a role and helps out. It's like a community service. We hang up decorations and lights. So much effort and hard work is put in by all the pumpkins that I have heard many say this serves as proof that we are indeed the second-hardest-working species in all the land, only behind ants. That's what I've been told, anyway.

We even make schedules for the consumption of the candy itself. Not one piece of candy is allowed to be eaten by any pumpkin until this whole process is complete. Last year, I watched the whole thing from afar, and it was very interesting. This year I was an active participant. I helped with the decorations. It took weeks of continuous work to sort it all out.

The excitement of going trick-or-treating had my stomach churning; there I lay awake in the middle of the night with no hope of falling asleep. I felt helpless. All my friends were probably asleep. My brother was asleep. He had fallen asleep hours ago.

Speaking of chocolate, I have a joke for you. Why did the M&M go to school? Because it wanted to be a Smartie.

Oh, my bad. Hello. I should introduce myself to you. Here I am, going on about how we store the Halloween candy, but you don't even know who I am. My name is Petrina Pumpkin. I am a four-year-old female. I have one brother; his name is Peter. He is also four years old. We were born on the same day. I could describe myself for you, but let's just say I look like a typical pumpkin. I am small, roundish, and orange, with vertical grooves that extend from the top of my head down to my waist. I could describe my personality to you, but there is nothing much to describe. I am your average, four-year-old female pumpkin, who acts, looks, talks, and thinks as you would expect, so I don't want to bore you with a lot of details about myself.

Besides, it was two days before Halloween. I think I said that already. I would have done anything to fall asleep. I felt like shaking my brother and waking him up and letting him know how excited I was, but he knew that already. I should let him sleep, anyway.

Peter said he was going to dress up as a ghost. I had decided to dress up as a witch—I think. Yes, most definitely a witch. Well, tomorrow I would decide for sure. Tomorrow would be costume day. My friend Pannette Pumpkin wanted to dress up as a person, like Goldilocks or Cinderella. Wow, a person. Imagine that. She hadn't decided which person yet.

Another close friend of mine, Pashelle Pumpkin, hadn't revealed her costume, as she wanted to keep it a secret. Pavneet Pumpkin was having difficulty deciding. She seemed all stressed-out about the whole choosing-a-costume exercise. We'd all decide once and for all the next day when we went into the city and brought those costumes home with us.

In the meantime, I couldn't fall asleep. Wow, this was painful.

My brother says that waiting for Halloween was going to be better than the actual trick-or-treating itself. My brother has a weird thought process. He thinks that the anticipation of an event is often better than the actual event itself—that when we go trick-or-treating, it won't be as much fun as we think it's going to be. I think that's kind of a negative view of life. It's like me thinking that waiting to fall asleep will be better than actually falling asleep. Oh, please. Give me a break. I believe the opposite. I believe that every day is the biggest day of your life. I like to live life in the moment.

Maybe Peter thinks this way because has no friends and nothing to look forward to. I think he has lots to look forward to. I mean, he might not have any friends, but he still has things to do that might excite him. Maybe he should come with us when we go out.

I should try not to think about anything, clear my head, and see if that works. Think blank space … not working. Let me try counting sheep. One … two … three … sleep … sleep … sleep.

 # CHAPTER 2
THE PATCH

What time was it? It was already eleven. I must have slept in. I almost always get up before eleven. I slept right through the morning. Oh, well. I should get myself fixed up, as today was going to be a busy day. We were going into the city to get our costumes.

I wondered what the weather was like. I got out of bed, onto my feet, and peered through the window of our brick house. It looked like it was about to rain. Or it had just rained because there were tiny puddles of water on the ground. Or maybe it was raining. The sky was full of clouds. I opened the front door and knelt down to feel the grass; it was soggy and wet. I guess the more important question is whether it was going to rain on Halloween. I hoped it didn't. I can handle the cold and wind, but not the rain. Even a little bit of rain makes my skin so soggy and wet that someone could use my skin to rinse off his or her hands.

All pumpkins beg for blue sky this time of year, I would imagine. The rain can be quite depressing because then we really can't go outside and play. We like to go outside, go hiking on the hills, or just play games. Once a year we go trick-or-treating, and the drier the better for us. We would have to see what the weather did as the day progressed. I will try to keep you updated as best I can.

Rise and shine, as they say. All the elders were awake, I'm sure, having prepared and eaten breakfast. I hardly ever wake up that early and have breakfast. For me, waking up early is always optional because I figure sleeping in can be good for you too. If I do get up early to have breakfast, I would normally drink coffee with toast. I love smelling fresh coffee beans. Elders say that most pumpkins develop a distaste for coffee as they grow older. I always eat lunch, though, and I was sure it was ready to be served by this time.

My brother had already left the house. The covers on his bed were neat and tidy. I should get myself together and head out to meet my friends for lunch. I washed my face, cleaned my body, tied on my blue bow, got my things together—which is pretty much nothing—and headed out the door for that long trek to the dining hall. Actually, it's not that long. It's only a twenty-minute walk.

I left the house, and walked north along column RY07, which is the column where Peter and I live. I met many other pumpkins along the way. I said hello to Pimi Pumpkin as soon as I got out the door. She lives with her two older sisters, next door to us, to the north. I pass by her quite a lot. She likes me. She is three years old. She's always asking me questions and wanting my advice on things that she needs help with.

There are 843 pumpkins that live on this Patch. There are many other Patches on the land. This is the fourth-largest out of a total of fourteen. The closest Patch from here is five cities away to the east of us. The largest Patch is miles away to the east, and it is almost ten times bigger than ours. The Grand Mr. Pumpkin lives on that Patch. I saw him once, when he visited our Patch last year.

Columns are walkways or paths. The ground beneath us is a combination of grass and dirt, as you can imagine. Our houses are on these paths. There are seventeen columns that stretch from the north down to the trees that border New Surrey City to the south.

Some columns do not stretch all the way south but instead merge with other columns. All the columns stretch vertically, north to south. There is one column—CC01—however, that extends diagonally from the schools in the northwest to a small, densely forested area in the southeast, providing an access channel for things like food distribution and communication.

Hundreds of years ago each column was designated by a two-digit letter, followed by a two-digit number, by some of the original pumpkins on this land, who thought that simplicity was best. As the tale goes, one old and deranged pumpkin was lost one day and couldn't recall where he lived, and all he could say was OI88. You see, he thought that some pumpkins were asking him if he had eaten dinner, and he kept saying, "Oh, I ate, ate." So when they finally decided to stop making fun of the old pumpkin, they escorted him home to a place called OI88, and thus the naming of the columns began. Actually, no pumpkin can really verify that, and it is only a rumor that has been passed down from generation to generation, but it makes for a good story nonetheless. Besides, I wasn't there at that time, was I?

As I continued to walk up column RY07, I noticed that the ground was getting soggier, and it made for a longer walk than usual. I was getting wet, not so much from the light drizzle falling from the sky, but from the water drops falling from the thick, overhanging evergreen bushes that separate this column from columns RY06 and RY08 to the east and west, respectively.

Giant redwood trees surround the Patch, providing a border from New Surrey City to the east and south, and smaller, thick oak trees border Burrowsville to the west. These trees can be up to five times as tall as the average trees on the land. Some say these trees can be up to two hundred feet tall and even double that size in the south. These trees are so tall that they serve as a defense system, providing protection from outside visitors. The trees are so tall that only the people's aircraft and the most skilled flying witches on their broomsticks can fly over them and see down onto the Patch.

Column RY07 merges to the right with RY06, which then merges with CD03. There are bushes on either side of RY07 and RY06, all the way up until they merge with CD03, and then all you can see is the magnificent Rose Garden up ahead, with the most beautiful and fragrant-smelling pink and red roses. Not today, though. It's too cold for those flowers to be blooming. Column CD03 is very wide all the way, with many columns merging into it, but as we walk up toward the Rose Garden, it narrows into a single-lane, S-shaped, curvy walking path. Once you pass a gate, the column branches out into many of these small single-lane walking paths that allow us to get up close to the flowers in the Rose Garden.

The gate is not really a physical gate where we open and close a fenced door, but more like an invisible boundary that separates this northern area from the rest of the Patch. This gate is called the West Gate. This northern area of the Patch is called the Eyepatch. It's called the Eyepatch because this is where many significant events in the Patch occur. Plus, it's also shaped like an eye. We actually refer to this area as simply the Eye. This area of the Patch is physically separated from the rest of the Patch by some of the most beautiful flower gardens in the land.

Apart from the kitchen and dining hall, in the Eye there is the hospital, the supply center, and an activity center. The kitchen and dining hall are actually located in the activity center. There is also a nice, comfy lounge in there, where my friends and I often meet up in the morning. There is also a large indoor arena, east of the activity center, with plenty of open space for games. It also serves as a meeting place for public announcements. In the northwest corner of the Eye, there is the office, where important decisions about the

Patch are made. There are currently thirty-one elders who meet in the office on a regular basis, and they discuss and decide on issues of importance to us all. An elder who meets in the office is called an Elected Elder. Elected Elders wear a star or badge on their right shoulder, so everyone knows who they are. Needless to say, the Eye is where the action is.

In the southwest corner of the Eye are the schools. We recognize the schools to be a part of the Eye, but they are actually located on the other side of the Tulip Garden, on the edge of Star River. Star River originates from a northern bay and flows through the farmlands, which are to the south of the schools, and then it flows parallel to column CC01 through the Patch. The river actually starts in Burrowsville. Here there is also a dam, which collects water in a reservoir for irrigation, drinking, and other uses. To access the schools from the Eye, we pass over a small walking bridge, and thus this gate is called the Water Gate. A golf course separates the schools and the farmlands. I don't play golf, but a lot of other pumpkins certainly do. The golf course is closed during the fall and winter.

As I continued to walk north on column CD03, through the Rose Garden, there was a mass of pumpkins assembled all over the Eye gardens. It seemed that each day this week, there were more and more pumpkins assembled here, as the excitement about Halloween continued to grow. I finally reached the large, wide entrance to the activity center. This entrance is called the main entrance. The Eye was a happening place today, that's for sure.

CHAPTER 3
THE EYEPATCH

Just as I was about to enter the center, I said hello to Mr. Pumpkin, who volunteers as a security guard. Security guards are some of the nicest pumpkins we will ever meet, probably because they always seem to be helping someone or coming to the rescue in one way or another. Guards serve all kinds of purposes. For instance, they monitor and supervise the people's sightseeing tours in the Patch. The young people, or children, are interested in the ways of our life, and so we let them come into the Patch from time to time to observe our activities. Most people are amazed and awed by our high work rate and good behavior. Well, maybe not mine, as I can tend to be a bit lazy at times, I must admit.

They are also intrigued by our communal way of life. Everything is shared by all of us. There are no possessions and no ownership of any property or objects, which is quite different from their way of life. Sightseeing tours are the only way people are allowed to enter the Patch. Other than that, there are only pumpkins here. The sightseeing tours do include visits to the Eye, and the most highly trained and skilled guards are specifically assigned to take care of just the Eye.

The sightseeing tours, moreover, are part of an agreement or understanding that we have with people. In exchange for allowing them to visit the Patch, they provide protection for us against the ghouls that terrorize us when we leave the Patch and enter the city. Just as there are pumpkin guards inside the Patch, there are people guards just on the outskirts of the Patch, in the city. If we are being attacked by a ghoul, then a person will assist us and help us to safety. It is also encouraged that, when we leave the Patch, we never travel alone but are always accompanied by other pumpkins, with a security guard. Pumpkin herds are when there are five or more pumpkins traveling together at one time.

As I entered the center, I headed straight to the posted sign-up sheet, near a temporary, makeshift tented area called Halloween Headquarters, to see what time we would start our adventure the next night. Plus I could confirm that my friends and I would be paired up as we intended. I pulled a copy down from the hanging pile on the bulletin board and began scanning the names on the list, searching for ours.

"Petrina! Petrina! Over here." It was Pannette Pumpkin, who had gotten up from her seat in the dining hall, which is just to the left as soon as you walk inside the main entrance. She had walked half the distance toward where I was standing and was calling me over. Pannette is one of my closest friends and has been since birth. In the seed chamber, Peter was to my right and Pannette to my left. I think she was the first pumpkin I said hello to. And we have been close ever since. She has two brothers, Patrick and Parson. They are both one year older. I don't talk to them very much, but I do notice that Patrick often performs very well in the school games. He is quite slim and athletic. I don't mind saying so. And his skin is a very nice shade of light-orange. Pannette is a more roundish pumpkin, which isn't much of a description, is it? It's like saying the person was slender. Aren't all people more slender than pumpkins? Well, not all people, I guess.

"We're going together! We got our pairing," she said excitedly, jumping up and down. I was still scanning the list of names to confirm this for myself.

"We're second to last," she said, trying to save me time, as I met her in the dining hall. She blurted out the secret before I had a chance to find out for myself. Everyone wants to be the bearer of good news. I flipped several pages until I reached the last page of the sign-up sheet. And there we were, listed in alphabetical order.

Group 41:
Pannette Pumpkin
Pashelle Pumpkin
Pavneet Pumpkin
Petrina Pumpkin
Plato Pumpkin
Polo Pumpkin

Well, this was great. This was really going to be fun.

"I know right," I said, pretending that I already knew.

There is no maximum number of pumpkins that can be paired together, but the total number must be manageable. One of the many rules we had to study. We had to take—and pass—a Halloween test with a score of at least 80 percent to be eligible to trick-or-treat. No one really fails because pumpkins can keep taking the test until we pass. It only took me four tries! That's kind of pathetic, I know. I hardly studied or paid attention in Halloween class. Most pumpkins pass the test on the second try, if not the first. I'm not sure what my problem was that day, but—whatever. I passed eventually. I'm actually pretty smart.

"And we're second to last," I added. "That's exciting!"

It might seem strange that first-years are the second to last to go out, it being very late and usually dark at about that time. It is quite practical, however. If all the younger pumpkins went out into the city all at the same time, that would mean too many young pumpkins out at the same time, all together. It becomes a safety issue. So the schedule is designed to alternate pairings with a group of younger pumpkins followed by a group of older ones followed by younger, then older, and so on. This way there is a balance of experience out in the city. The purpose of which is that the older ones can help the younger ones if there is some kind of a problem. This was all explained to us in Halloween class. There are elders who do volunteer and stay on the streets while we are in the city. And people do help protect us, but not as much as you might think. We try to take every precaution we can.

I was still scanning through the sheet to see what order everyone was in. Party, Payne, and Perry would leave just before us. And Pod and Pol, who have asterisks next to their names, are the last ones to leave the Patch. They have those asterisks because they are seniors, or pumpkins who are in their final year of trick-or-treating. This year, like all years, the seniors will be honored after trick-or-treating in the closing ceremony. This year, there are twenty-seven seniors.

As Pannette and I approached the seats where Pannette had been sitting, Pashelle managed to swallow what she was eating, got up from her seat, and was poised to give me a high five, but I pretended to have too many papers in my hands, rejected her gesture, and then sat down. A joke on her can be so satisfying because she is always playing jokes on everyone else.

"I'm joking … a high five to you," I said, holding my hand way up in the air. She instead gave me a kiss on the cheek, whispered, "I'll get you back," and sat back down on the other side of the table.

"Okay, so what's the plan for today?" she finally said, after all the pumpkins sitting at the table who had watched me tease her, had stopped laughing. The dining tables are quite long, as each table can seat twenty-two.

"How come you're not in the lounge?" I asked, wondering why everyone was in here, munching away on food.

"It's too crowded," I heard a few pumpkins at the table respond.

"Where's Pavneet?" I asked, searching the hall. I thought that I had arrived late this morning.

"She still isn't feeling well," replied Pannette. "When I woke up, I went to her house. And she is normally awake really early in the morning, right? But she wasn't even there. She was actually walking really slowly back to her house. She didn't even tell me where she went. She said she just went outside to get some fresh air. She must have gotten up really early, too. She still looks so pale. So I thought, okay, well, just come back in and lie in bed for a while and see if you feel better. Because if Ms. Pumpkin finds out that she is sick, then she may not even be allowed to go out tomorrow."

Good idea, I thought. Pannette has always been quick on her feet, coming up with solutions in a jiffy to problems, or potential problems.

"Did you feel her skin?" I asked.

"Why would I feel her skin?" she asked.

"To see if she was really sick."

"What did I just say?" she asked me again.

"Yeah, I know what you said, but didn't you feel her skin?"

"I don't need to feel someone's skin to see if she is sick."

"Okay, okay," I conceded. I would have definitely felt her skin, just to see how soft it was and to get a better idea of how sick she really was.

"Who cares if Pannette felt her skin? What are we going to do now? When are we going to get our costumes?" asked Pashelle. She was getting anxious about her costume, which was still supposed to be a surprise.

As Pannette started talking about our schedule, my mind was still on the sign-up sheet and how come I could not find Peter. I had gone through this thirteen-page list three times, and no Peter. It was like he didn't even submit his name or something. It's not mandatory to submit your name to go out trick-or-treating. If you don't, then you get assigned with the communal group. The communal group members, I was told, would be listed on the final pages, but for some reason, the communal group members were not attached to this sheet. So I grabbed a sign-up sheet from another pumpkin across from another table.

"Hey there," that pumpkin objected.

"Just wait. I need to see something." I flipped through the communal listing, and there he was. Well, I guess this was not surprising. Peter didn't have any friends. I know that's kind of a mean thing to say, but I'm telling the truth. I've always had to be bossy with my brother, and I'm never sure exactly why. I've always had to help him do everything. He can be so useless sometimes. Do you know one time he apparently lost his glasses, and because he is so blind, he went into a stranger's house. Like how long does it take to figure out that you are in someone else's house? Well, he was there for hours, and we all thought he was lost. He was nowhere to be found, until the pumpkins next door went home at night … and lo and behold, there he was, just sitting there. Doing nothing. He can be an accident waiting to happen. One time I was sitting next to him in the dining hall, and another pumpkin flung some cabbage in an attempt to hit Peter right in the face. He missed, and it got me right on the chin. I can tell you it can be dangerous, too.

I've always told him to be more social and to try to make friends, but it's like he doesn't care if he does or doesn't. He's a loner and doesn't try to talk to anyone. I think life is too short to go through it without having friends, or even worse, not even trying to make friends. Pumpkins need other pumpkins to talk to and share things with. We naturally need to be with each other. We are a social species. So how he does it, I will never know. The thing is that he is quiet and shy and keeps to himself. He goes through life speaking only when he has to. And so if he's in the communal group, then good, I thought. He has a chance to make new friends by going out to trick-or-treat with different pumpkins, as opposed to trying to hang around me and my friends all the time.

"Well, Petrina ... what type of witch?" repeated Plato, apparently for the third time. And it broke my concentration.

"Just wait a second."

I didn't want Peter to go in the communal group after all. It was just better if he came with us. He should come with us, I convinced myself. He is my brother. And besides, this is probably the best way I can keep track of him.

So I got up from my chair and walked out of the dining hall and back toward Halloween Headquarters. This was where we would report when it was our time to go out the next day. This was our first check-out point. Our journey would start from here. I got a change slip from the counter, wrote Peter's name as a delete from the communal group, then wrote his name as an addition to Group 41, and handed the slip to Ms. Pumpkin.

"What have we here? It's a change. Oh, Petrina, isn't that splendid? Peter has decided to come with you," she concluded.

He's decided? No, I decided. Why would she think this was his decision? I'm the one who's being nice to him.

"So let me just make note of this change, and we'll be set to go," she said. She wasn't sure whether or not I needed Peter's approval, and so she turned to ask another Ms. Pumpkin.

"Polly? Someone has submitted a change slip on behalf of some-one else. Does the first pumpkin need to approve?"

The question didn't seem to make any sense. The other Ms. Pumpkin replied that it was probably okay. Wasn't there a procedure already in place for this type of request? Didn't Ms. Pumpkin know what to do? Didn't they have to pass a test?

Anyways, I didn't care, as I had achieved my objective. And then I hurried back to the dining hall table, which essentially meant pushing my way through the pumpkins near the main entrance. The main entrance is really a door, but we also refer to it as the whole area when you come inside the center. It's more like a lobby or greet-ing area than just a door.

"Where did you just go?" asked Pashelle.

"I went to the tent. Peter's coming with us," I announced, expect-ing to hear moans and groans. "I know, I know, you're thinking that I'm being overly nice, but I think this is better."

"Okay, great." At least Polo was being nice. As a matter of fact, they all seemed pleased and broke out in surprising smiles. Well, they didn't have to be that nice, either.

Speaking of Peter, he had just come into the dining hall by him-self, and was waiting in line to get lunch. Oh, I had actually forgotten to get any food. The rice and yogurt really smelled nice. The special of the day was spaghetti, with a marinated clam sauce. And garlic bread. From looking around at the various trays and plates on the surrounding tables, I could see that other sorts of pasta were also on the menu. I saw plates full of penne and lasagna. Polo was eating spaghetti, but he had separated out the noodles and was only inter-ested in the giant meatballs. Everything smelled so good. Wouldn't it be great if I became a gourmet chef, when I grew up? Anything and everything would be so good if I learned how to cook. I should talk to the head chef one day. I could still get in line now, if I wanted.

I should at least get my morning coffee. No, never mind. I guessed I was not that hungry. Besides, my friends were almost finished with their meals, and who knew if they would even wait up for me?

"Hey, Peter," I heard some pumpkins say, as he passed right by us and sat down next to Porter at the adjacent table. Porter was sitting by himself as well, so now they both had company. Porter immediately went for Peter's glasses and began cleaning them. They were dirty. He must have fallen down somewhere along the way to the Eye. I had noticed Porter's name in the communal group as well.

I tried to get Peter's attention by waving and holding up my arms, but he wasn't noticing my effort, so I yelled out over the raucous noise of pumpkins talking about costumes. "Peter, you're coming with me!" He seemed to be scanning the list, himself. This time I was the bearer of good news.

"No. Wait a minute," he objected, but I think that inside he felt relieved that he was coming with us. His voice can sound like such a monotone sometimes, with no expression, so it can be difficult to gauge any emotions by his body language.

He can say something so exciting yet have such a tired look on his face. And other times, he can say something so stupid or strange or quirky with such elation on his face, apparently thinking it can get a conversation going or something. Sometimes his words can tell a story, but other times they can be meaningless, though his face could paint a thousand words. He's kind of an enigma. No one really knows him.

Peter is about my height, which is 2 feet 1 inch. We don't grow any taller after we turn six years old. He is a little heavier, but not by very much. Not really noticeable. He wears glasses. He is the only pumpkin I have ever heard of wearing glasses at such a young age. He kept misplacing things and could never locate anything, even when sometimes it was right in front of his face. So Dr. Pumpkin made him take an eye exam, and he failed it last year, and so the doctor prescribed glasses. He has to wear them everywhere he goes, but you can tell that he doesn't like to wear them.

His skin color is a dull orange, but still a very strong and dark orange. His skin is very hard. He has no marks or wounds on his skin, despite having serious walking issues. I don't mean to say he limps or anything. It's just that he stumbles a lot, especially when he tries to walk fast. He has fallen down right on his face so many times, the ground beneath his feet braces for a thud when he comes its way. His mind is hard and thick also, in the sense that nothing seems to faze him. As I've said before, he is a loner. He gets picked on a lot, by all sorts of creatures—pumpkins, people, and ghouls alike. They make jokes about him. Like 'Peter, Peter, pumpkin eater, had a wife and couldn't keep her.' That one doesn't even make sense, as Peter is only four years old. He's not even married, let alone separated or divorced from a wife.

'Peter, Peter, pumpkin eater, got out of bed but always a dreamer.' Well, that one is probably true. He always seems to have a confused look on his face.

'Peter, Peter, pumpkin eater, wrote a test but always a cheater.' Well, I don't think he cheated on his trick-or-treat test, and he doesn't go to school full-time until next year.

'Peter, Peter, pumpkin eater, tried to run, never passed a meter.' I heard that one when he was playing soccer the other day. He certainly does not run very fast and is not very athletic.

'Peter, Peter, pumpkin eater, kept a secret by being a squealer.' That one is lame.

'Peter, Peter, pumpkin eater, found a rat then tried to feed her.' I heard that one just last week, and that was directed at me. I don't eat rat, and I don't think he would feed me rat to begin with.

As many of those Peter Pumpkin jokes as I have heard, I bet he has heard ten times more than me. And the whole premise of the joke doesn't even make sense. I mean, Peter does not eat pumpkin. None of us do. We don't eat rat, and we don't eat pumpkin. That is gross. That's like cannibalism. No pumpkin eats pumpkin!

But he is so internally strong that those jokes almost go in one ear and out the other. Maybe it's because there is nothing inside his head, like he has no brain. How about this one: 'Peter, Peter, pumpkin eater, tried to learn but is no keener.' That was funny. Oh, my bad. I shouldn't be laughing at him.

He did seem a bit surprised by my announcement. He got up and took a few steps toward our table.

"No, Petrina, I signed up with the communal group," he protested.

I started laughing. "You signed up in that group? Why didn't you just ask me, and you could have just come with us? Talk to me, Peter, I'm your sister. I'm supposed to help you any way I can."

"But I already promised Ms. Pumpkin. You should have asked me first. Now what am I going to do?"

I thought to myself that he was being very ungrateful. I turned my attention to my friends and couldn't be bothered with his sniveling.

"Oh, come on. Let's get out of here," I said as I got up, trying to get out of Peter's way. This was going to be a very busy day, after all.

"Peter, I'm smarter than you. You should listen to me more," I said to him, trying to end the subject. I wasn't bragging or anything. I was just trying to be honest. Sometimes you have to tell someone exactly how it is, or else they will never learn. Do you know what I mean?

"If there is no room in the lounge, then let's go to Pannette's. And we can check up on Pavneet along the way," I suggested.

"Bye, Peter," I heard my friends say. I couldn't believe how ungrateful Peter was and how selfish he was being, but I was not going to let that ruin my day.

Pannette, Pashelle, Polo, Plato, and I walked out of the dining hall, out of the activity center, out through the Rose Garden, past the West Gate, and south on Column CD03. From there, it does not take long to take the exit path east that leads to Column TY07, which is where Pannette and Pavneet live. Not together, I mean, but they both live on TY07. We left Peter behind to do his own thing, whatever that was.

I know I touched upon the Patch earlier, but I should try to diagram it better for you, so you can get an idea of where we are and where we are going.

The Patch is surrounded by two cities. Burrowsville is to the left, or west of us. New Surrey City, one of the largest cities in the land, is to the south and east. To the north is water, which is called Burnaby Bay. Way out into the bay, you can see Romo Island. Few people actually live on this island, but many people do go visit. You can take a boat and tour this island. There are some nice gardens, where you can examine flowers and other types of fauna and foliage, we are told. There is a large botanical garden. The only people who live on this island are gardeners and scientists. Apparently, this is a place where people like to do experiments and testing for things that might make their lives better. No pumpkin has ever traveled to this island, not that we know of, as we don't think any pumpkin would feel comfortable on a boat for the two-hour ferry ride. Boats are not always safe, and, as you know, pumpkins don't swim.

The Eye borders on Burnaby Bay. Of course, you cannot see the Eye from the Bay because of the tall, thick trees, but you can see the water by passing the office, climbing up a small hill, and then sticking your head out between the trees. We call these trees Eyelashes. Not only because they are really pretty, but because they are geographically located at the top of the Eye. I have always wanted to see the water up close, just out of curiosity more than anything, but this is not something I am holding my breath to do. Way off in the distance, there are the Aikman Islands, but they are not visible from this vantage point. Past the Aikman Islands, there is only water, for miles and miles.

It would take a pumpkin just over an hour to walk from the northern tip of the Eye to the southern border of New Surrey City. And it would take a pumpkin just under two hours to walk from the eastern border of New Surrey City to the western border of Burrowsville.

Much of Burrowsville is farmland. The western part of the Patch is also farmland. Many of the pumpkins volunteer as farmers, growing fruits and vegetables. Engineers closely monitor the reservoir and dam, in cooperation with the people in Burrowsville, although the people do most of the repairs and upgrades required. The farmland does extend to Burnaby Bay, but only from Burrowsville. Pumpkin engineers ensure that we have enough clean water to drink. Pumpkins for the most part are vegetarian, although it is not forbidden for us to eat meat. Some pumpkins do eat chicken. I have tried it, but I don't always like it. We grow all our own food.

To the east of the Eye is a large hill. I love this hill. It's my favorite spot in the whole world. I love going up this hill. The hill is quite steep, so I have to be careful not to trip and fall. It's actually easier and safer climbing up the hill than coming down. I did fall coming down the hill once and scraped my knee against a rock. I couldn't imagine actually losing my balance and falling all the way down. Any slipup could result in a long, deadly fall. Atop the hill, after you manage to squeeze past the trees, you come to a cliff. And from this cliff, there is an incredible view.

You are high enough to get a clear picture of Burnaby Bay and Romo Island to the left. And you can see the tall city buildings in the city to the right. You can almost look down onto the city from there and see the people in their cars. You can see their houses, some big and some small. There is nothing like that in the Patch. At night, the glow of the building lights reflects off the water. From this view, you can see that the city is constructed quite differently compared to the Patch, if anyone had any doubts. In the patch, the houses look the same in style, shape, and color. Even the larger houses are not that much bigger. It's a symbol to us that all pumpkins are the same and should be treated equally. Or maybe it's because the Patch engineers lacked any sort of imagination during construction. I choose to accept the former explanation.

It seems so peaceful, yet so dangerous and scary on that hill at the same time. The cliff itself doesn't really have a name, so I call it Petrina's hill. Why not, right? Generally speaking, we are advised never to go onto the cliff because it's assumed that if the Patch ever came under attack by the ghouls, this would be their landing point from up above. This is where they would approach from. This is the only area of the Patch where someone can land from the sky without having to soar over the trees. Although this cliff is dangerous to land on because of its jagged nature and uneven surfacing and small space, all other areas of the Patch are protected by tall trees. Theoretically, someone can land on this cliff and make their way downhill, through the trees, and into the confines of the Patch. Moreover, a witch can swoop in and pick up an unsuspecting pumpkin who is on this cliff. I go to this cliff when I want to be alone.

The rest of the Patch is considered residential. It's where we all live in our brick houses. As we walked south on Column TY07, I noticed that someone had planted higher shrubs there. Not planted, per se, because obviously they take a while to grow tall. But had installed or placed them in the ground. Why did they do that? How come my column didn't get this upgrade? That's not really fair. The shrubs and bushes on column RY07 are in much worse condition than the ones that were here before. Oh well. No big deal. That must have been this morning because I didn't notice them yesterday. The columns are divided by fresh, very green-looking shrubs. Some are higher than others, and these new ones are much higher than the previous ones.

We don't have far to walk along TY07 until we reach Pavneet's house. She lives very close to the Eye. Many of us envy this close proximity to the Eye. Only the lucky ones, I guess.

CHAPTER 4
GOOD AFTERNOON

"Pavneet are you home?" we shouted, as we knocked on the door. "Come in. Yes. I was just getting ready and coming to meet you guys. When are we going to get our costumes?" she replied when she opened the door.

"Are you sure it's a good idea for you to come with us today? I mean, Pavneet, have you looked in the mirror? You have almost no orange left on your body," I told her.

"Ssssshhhhh!" she said discreetly, yet loudly at the same time. "They're home." She was referring to her roommates. Pavneet does not have any brothers or sisters, so she lives with another family of four. So five pumpkins in this house altogether. They are never nice to her. They treat her like an outsider. They make her feel as if she is some kind of an alien, in her own home. Her roommates are much older and have lived in this house for a very long time, before Pavneet was even born. And they objected to her moving in right from the get-go.

One time, Pavneet told us the story of how she left the house without cleaning up after herself and how they locked her out when she returned and left her outside for half the night. Can you believe that? And they said that if she ever complained, they would make her life even more miserable. So she has never complained or voiced any negative feelings toward them. Isn't that mean? They make her clean the whole house by herself all the time, for weeks on end, just to teach her lessons. I could never handle some of the things that she has had to go through, and the situation keeps getting worse for her as each month passes by. She has requested a transfer to another house, and I think the Elected Elders are going to conduct a hearing and make a decision about her housing situation. Very soon, I hope, for her sake. I have told the Elected Elders that she would be more than welcome to stay with Peter and me. It would be nice to have another household member. Talking to Peter can get quite boring.

She stepped outside. "I know. But I think I'm okay. I don't feel very tired anymore," she said, as she started walking toward the Eye, waiting for us to follow her.

We stared at each other, half in denial, wanting to hold her back for the day's events, but it was not likely that we were going to convince her that she should be cooped up in her house all day while we went into the city and had a blast. She is the most social and outgoing of all my friends. What am I saying? She is the most outgoing pumpkin I have ever, and will ever, meet. She loves to go hiking and comes with me on treks up Petrina's hill. She loves playing sports. She is very fit and athletic. She loves the outdoors and does not like to stay in very much at all. If there was a choice to do an activity inside or outside, she would choose the outside activity every time, no matter the weather or the conditions.

"I'm going today. And I'm not arguing with you about this." She waited a second before she added an "okay?" And it wasn't really a question, either.

"This way, Pavneet. Don't go near any elder. Stay in hiding, away from everyone," Polo suggested.

We weren't going to change her mind, so we continued our walk south without going inside her house.

Pannette lives only six houses south of Pavneet, so it doesn't take long for us to go back and forth between Pavneet's and Pannette's. We tend to hang out at one house or the other, whichever is empty. Polo and Plato live quite far, as they are southwest of the Eye, in Column DS14, and about thirty houses south. Pashelle is three columns to the east of me, on Column CD04, but also quite a ways south. Don't ask me why CD03 and CD04 are not next to each other because I have no idea. Pashelle has quite a walk to get to the Eye, so we never really go to her place. Besides she has four brothers and two sisters who are always home, so we never really get any privacy. We only go there when we really want to party. Despite the fact that it's quite a ways away from the Eye, a lot of pumpkins get together there, as a party house. Maybe because if it's far for us to walk, it's also far for the elders to walk. The place is rarely subjected to surprise inspections.

Each house almost has the same design inside. There are sitting rooms and washrooms and bedrooms. The houses in Columns CD03, CD04, and CD05 are more spacious, to accommodate larger families.

When we arrived at Pannette's, we went inside and sat down.

"Do they know?" Someone had to ask whether her roommates knew she was sick.

"I don't think so. They never notice anything about me, so I doubt it."

"What did you eat, anyway? You must have eaten some rotten food. When did you start getting sick? You seemed okay before."

"I don't want to think about it, to be honest."

"Did you eat the spinach and potatoes and the bread from the oven? Maybe the spinach was bad. Or maybe the potatoes were bad."

"Potatoes are never bad."

"How do you know?"

"If they were bad, then how come no one else got sick?"

"Maybe she is just sick—just because she is sick. Has anyone thought of that? I mean, pumpkins do get sick. The weather has changed. I mean, just a few weeks ago it was sunny and warm. And look how cold it is today."

Plato had a good point. That was possible. But it didn't make any sense to me. Pavneet lives a healthy lifestyle. She is a health nut and keeps herself in terrific condition. I'm in great condition as well, if you are wondering. But I must admit, Pavneet is extraordinary in this regard.

"What does everyone want to do?" Polo interjected.

"Let's play cards," Pashelle suggested.

"Let's play hide and seek."

"Let's practice trick-or-treating."

"That's stupid. We don't have any candy to give out."

"We can use play candy. And don't call me stupid." Plato hated when someone called him stupid. Even as a joke. It seemed like each day he was becoming smarter, compared to the rest of us.

"We don't need to practice. Besides, that's boring."

And so our idle chatter went on. We can talk for hours with each other about meaningless subjects that no other pumpkin would even care about.

I didn't care what we did … I was just waiting for our call to go into the city to get our costumes. I was just killing time.

"Let's play cards," repeated Pashelle, tiring of the idle chatter.

She likes to play cards, and since she is the bossy one, we tend to let her do her thing. She picked up the deck of cards that was on the table and began dealing. We play lots of different card games. The easiest and simplest of which is a game we call blackjack. Initially two cards are dealt, and the closest person to have their cards add up to twenty-one points wins the game. You can have as many cards as you want, after the initial two are given. But if you go over twenty-one, you lose.

"Did you take any medicine?" asked Pannette, not wanting to change the subject.

"I don't have any," replied Pavneet.

"You told me you did," Pannette pointed out.

"No, I didn't. I said that I have lots of blankets. You didn't even ask me if I had any medicine."

"Because I knew you didn't." Pannette took out a small bottle from inside her sac and held it up in the air. "Look what I got." They were medicine pills.

"Where did you get those?"

"Don't ask. But I have them."

"Give me one," Polo requested.

"No. This is medicine, stupid. They're only for Pavneet."

"But if they can make Pavneet feel better, they can make me feel better too."

"Why? What's wrong with you?"

"Like, have you seen his face lately?" Pashelle couldn't resist.

"I know, right," I confirmed, wanting to play along.

"What do you know, right? What's wrong with my face?"

"It's all pressed in. Did you get hit by a soccer ball or something?" I wanted to see his reaction.

"His face is always like that. It's like someone is inside your body and is trying to suck your face inward," Pashelle explained.

"Oh, you're so funny, Pashelle."

Sometimes we can talk so fast, with everyone talking at the same time, that it's hard to remember who said what.

"Good. Let me take one pill. I need to get better. I was so tired when I woke up this morning," Pavneet agreed, going to the kitchen to get a glass of water, and swallowing the pill that Pannette had given her. She never took a drink of the water, though. Wow, she swallowed medicine without taking a sip of water! Is she Wonder Woman, or something?

"Are you Wonder Woman or something? Drink some water. It might get stuck in your throat."

Pashelle looked angrily at me, as if I had uncovered some kind of secret.

"Blackjack! So that's three for me so far," exclaimed Pashelle. Meaning that Pashelle had won three times so far. Sometimes we sort of play for real, in that whoever gets the most wins in one day gets to boss everyone else around. And Pashelle is the most eager to play and wins the most, and that's why she becomes so bossy. We can never tell if she is being bossy because she got the most wins from the card game the previous day or just because she likes to tell other people what to do. When you get an ace and a face card, then you say "blackjack," and you win that game.

"How did you get that bottle of medicine?"

"Well, it was by mistake, almost. This morning I walked by the school soccer field, and someone kicked the ball just as I was walking by the goal net. It hit me in the stomach. I wasn't even paying attention. Mr. Pumpkin saw, and he asked if I was hurt. And I was about to say no, but then I thought I could see what type of medicine we have in the hospital. So I said I was in pain. Mr. Pumpkin took me to the hospital and said to Ms. Pumpkin that I needed some pain relief. Well, when I got there, the medicine cabinet was already open. And as they were talking and not paying any attention, I took this bottle."

"You stole it?"

"I cannot believe you stole this."

"Aw!" I exclaimed, looking at Pannette with some degree of amazement. Wow. Pannette had guts to do that.

"I didn't steal it. I'm just borrowing it for a few days, and then I'll put it back."

"And how are you going to put it back?"

"The same way I took it. I'm going to get hit by another soccer ball and make another trip to the hospital. No one is going to find out."

"What type of medicine is this? What did I just eat? Are you saying that Dr. Pumpkin didn't prescribe this?"

"All medicine is the same."

"No, it's not. There are different medicines for different things."

"Well, I think you're going to feel better soon," Pannette said confidently. She was almost convinced there weren't going to be any further health issues.

I wasn't convinced. "Did anyone bother to read the instructions label? Let me see." I found myself fighting with Pavneet and Pashelle for the bottle. Pashelle got control of it, got up off her seat to get some separation from us, and began reading.

A few seconds passed. "Well, what does it say?"

"Take two tablets every six hours. That's all it says."

"Oh, my God. What did I just swallow?" asked Pavneet after she had gotten control of the bottle. "That's all it says. Take two tablets every six hours?" Pavneet had a very worried, confused look on her face.

"Give it to me." After I got control of the bottle, I began looking for small print. There certainly was lots of wording on this bottle. And most of them were very long words that I didn't recognize and were difficult to pronounce. Diphenhydramine. Benadryl. Unisom. Sominex. What do these mean? And the bottle didn't indicate why someone should take this medicine or what it exactly fixes.

"Pannette, like I'm thinking this wasn't such a great idea. What if these pills actually make her sicker and then she can't go trick-or-treating at all?"

"I've heard of the word Sominex, but I can't quite recall what it is … I think that …"

"Just relax, okay? Everything is going to be fine," said Pannette, interrupting Plato. She was trying to reassure all of us. She herself began to read some of the ingredients, but she had no more knowledge about them than the rest of us.

"Just take it back, Pannette," I suggested.

Although she was still convinced that taking the medicine from the hospital and feeding it to Pavneet was a good idea, she did realize that taking unknown medicine could potentially have made Pavneet worse. So she reluctantly agreed to take the medicine back as soon as she could. How she was going to do this, I wasn't sure. We decided to come up with some ideas and the sooner the better.

Pavneet spent the rest of the afternoon lying down, feeling tired, and then eventually fell asleep on the couch. We continued to play cards. I could imagine how she felt. If I was her, I wouldn't even have tried to sleep at that point. I mean, what would happen if she didn't wake up? Put away those tragic thoughts, Petrina, and think more positively.

"So you never answered me from before. Are you still going be a witch?" asked Pashelle.

"Yes, I think so. Maybe I'll dress up like Wanda Witch," I finally answered.

There was a collective "oooh" from the room. What a dangerous thing to go out as—Wanda Witch. The pumpkins' most feared ghoul is Wanda Witch.

I corrected myself. "Actually I'm going to be a good witch. If there is such a thing. A good but scary witch."

"We should all go as witches. Can you imagine?"

"I'm not dressing up as a witch. That's a girl's costume. I'm Superman. And Plato is going as Batman," announced Polo.

"You're going as a man bat?" Pashelle was teasing.

"Haven't you heard of Batman? He's a superhero."

"There's no such thing as Batman. He's a made-up superhero, not a real one. Same with Superman. He doesn't really exist."

"So? That doesn't matter. I can be anything I want to be."

"I will be Cinderella. I'll find the fanciest dress ever." Pannette had wanted to be Cinderella since the day she was born. "And I need to make sure I get the right shoes, too."

"Why. What's with the shoes?" Pashelle was teasing again.

"It's the shoes that make her meet up with the prince. Oh, don't give me that. You've read the story of Cinderella."

"Did you hear Pandora go on earlier? 'Oh what about me? I still don't know what to be. I'm so undecided. Give me some ideas.' We've given her a million ideas for months now, and she still acts like she doesn't know. Like give me a break." Pashelle had never liked Pandora.

"Ever since she found that box, she's been acting so strange."

This was true. Wandering around the wooded area southeast of the Patch a few months back, she had found a box. She claimed that a ghost-like creature was standing over it, and the ghost said, "Hold on to this box, but never, ever open it. No matter what. Bad things will happen if you do." So we sometimes try to trick her into opening the box, but she is steadfast and won't play along. Wasn't she the slightest bit curious about what was in this box she lugged around all day? And why was she in that wooded area in the first place? What a weird place to be. There's nothing there to see, except some wild animals, which may or may not be dangerous.

"She should go out as a cat. She likes animals." Then I changed the subject. I mean, who cares about Pandora, anyway. "If Pavneet doesn't come with us tonight, we'll get her the princess costume ..."

Just then a knock on the door changed my thoughts. "Quick, open the door. Is everyone ready to go?"

Pannette raced to the door and flung it wide open. It was Mr. Pumpkin. What a surprise! But he didn't give us our okay to leave the Patch. Instead he asked Pashelle to come to the office. Why did Pashelle have to go to the office? This was sudden.

"This is a waste of time, Mr. Pumpkin. I cannot believe that any-one is actually taking this seriously," Pashelle said to him.

"What's going on?" I asked.

"I'll tell you after. But everything is okay. Nothing happened. Just trust me." And Mr. Pumpkin led Pashelle out of the house.

"Come and get me when you guys go out tonight," she managed to say before leaving and closed the door behind her.

We stared at each other, almost in shock. That scene had hap-pened so fast. It was like Pashelle was almost expecting it. Actually, shock might not be the right word. Well, we were in shock because of the timing of the summons. But this was not the first time she had been called into the office. As a matter of fact, it was starting to become a regular occurrence for her. She can be so sassy and lippy. Sometimes she shows no respect. No regard for other pumpkins' feelings. She had to go to the office just last week because she told Portia that Parker was looking for her, and that it was urgent, and sent her on a wild-goose chase. And then told Parker the same thing. That Portia was looking for him and sent him in the complete oppo-site direction. This was right after Parker told Pashelle that he was not interested in becoming Pashelle's friend. Why does Pashelle play these silly games? I must admit, though, it was funny, and we all got a kick out of it.

"I think I know why she's in trouble."

Polo began to tell us what he knew but then hesitated. Polo is very outgoing and personable. He doesn't speak very often, but he should. He's smart. A very easygoing, mild-mannered, polite, and funny pumpkin, and he always speaks confidently when he has something important to say. But this time he seemed to be waiting for us to encourage him to pass on the information.

"Yes, okay, Polo. What do you know?"

"I was talking to Peter yesterday, and he was telling me that Pashelle might be in trouble. That we all might be in trouble."

What did he mean?

"Hey, look. I didn't do anything wrong," I said.

"Yeah, me neither," said Pannette.

"Pashelle made a deal with Wanda Witch."

"What?"

Wanda Witch is the leader of the witches. She commands, and most all other witches follow. She is one of the few ghouls with such a powerful broomstick that she can soar over the trees and see below into the Patch. She doesn't have any special powers, except for that very powerful broomstick. Wanda claimed it was handed down to her voluntarily by Wynona Witch. That Wanda was the chosen one and would be a better leader of all the witches. But everyone knows that is not the way it all went down. That broomstick was not handed over voluntarily.

As it was explained to us, the real story is that Wanda and her band of rebels revolted against the witch leadership and killed Wynona Witch in the famous War of the Broomsticks. This was not long ago. Once the witch leadership was destroyed, all the witches either had to side with Wanda or fight against her. The war that ensued affected ghouls, people, and pumpkins alike. All species. Even animals. There were hundreds and hundreds of ghouls fighting. People tried to stay neutral during this war, but a lot of them died and were wounded anyway. Many people suffered heart attacks and strokes. Even though pumpkins were also neutral, the war affected this Patch directly, as the fighting spread over to much of the land. It left much of this Patch in ruins.

After Wanda seized control of the witch leadership, she attacked the Patch, and many pumpkins died. She has never liked pumpkins. As a matter of fact, she loves to hate us. She will do anything to make our lives difficult. It's a wonder to us because we have never done anything to harm her. The people were forced to make a peace agreement with her when the war ended. The President of the land kept insisting they didn't make deals with terrorists, without suggesting that Wanda was a terrorist. But if something looks like a chicken and talks like a chicken and acts like a chicken, then it is a chicken. Do you know what I mean? Things were peaceful between ghouls and people for hundreds of years, until Wanda came along. She claimed the broomstick was her birthright. The people were almost forced to acknowledge Wanda as the leader. Each side has kept up its side of the peace bargain ever since. For the most part, ghouls try to avoid any direct contact with people and vice versa. There has not been a major war since, but Wanda is always on the prowl for our candy. She always seems to be looking for trouble.

"What deal?" I pressed Polo.

"Pashelle made an agreement with Wanda Witch. Wanda is going to give Pashelle a broomstick, and Pashelle is going to tell Wanda where we're going to store the candy from this year's trick-or-treating," explained Polo.

"Peter said this?" I was alarmed.

"No. He just told me about it. It was Panic that is making the claim. Panic is saying that Wanda knows where we're going to keep the candy," Polo clarified.

"That's not true. Pashelle wouldn't say anything to Wanda about that. Not just for a stupid broomstick." Pannette was in disbelief. Even for Pashelle, this was way over the line.

"But what if it's true? Pashelle would be a traitor. She's always saying she would do anything to get her hands on a magical broomstick. That she would love to fly among the witches and soar over all the land," said Plato.

I did not believe it for a second. Panic was being an idiot, I thought. And so was everyone else.

"Panic is being an idiot. Like how does he know?" I asked.

"If I had a broomstick, I would fly all over the world. Anyone would want one," argued Plato. Neither Polo nor Plato was sure what to believe.

"I don't. I don't like flying. I'm afraid of heights," confessed Polo.

Really? Polo is afraid of heights? That really cute pumpkin doesn't like to go up in the sky and look down? I'd always wanted to spend some time with him on Petrina's Hill, but now I wondered if he would come up there with me. I might have to rethink my strategy with him. In case you haven't realized, I kind of liked him.

"Why does she always say that she wishes she had a broomstick, then? If Wanda is willing to give her one, then Pashelle would need to offer something in return," reasoned Plato.

"Yeah, like tell her where all our candy will be?" asked Pannette.

"What do you think—that Wanda has all of these spare broomsticks stuffed away in her closet ready to be given away?" I asked sarcastically. Then I thought to myself, Yes, she probably does have lots of spare broomsticks.

"So that's why Ms. Pumpkin was giving a speech this morning, reminding us about the importance of unity and sticking together. And never to go near any ghouls, especially Wanda Witch," said Pannette.

Not all ghouls are evil, only Wanda and those truly loyal to her.

Most ghouls just like to scare us and play mean tricks on us. But taking our candy is evil. If Wanda had her way, she would exterminate all pumpkins.

"When was this?" I inquired.

"Like when you were sleeping."

"Oh."

"You never come to any of the morning announcements."

"Petrina sleeps in so many times, she thinks she's a bat," said Plato.

"That's stupid. Is that supposed to be funny?" I wasn't expecting an answer.

"Wait a minute. How does Panic know this?" Pannette still had questions.

"Nobody knows for sure. He's just saying," replied Polo.

"What if it's true that the witches are going to take our candy?"

"The elders are not going to let that happen. You know the candy is kept safe, hidden under lock and key," I said.

"I'm scared, Polo," Plato admitted.

The theory has always been that Wanda would never invade the Patch without knowing where the candy is. An invasion without knowing would cause an unnecessary time delay for her. By the time she found the candy, we would have had enough time to organize our forces and be able to defend ourselves. We would have enough time to seek assistance from people, as part of our agreement with them. But if she knew where it was, she could mount a surprise attack, probably from Petrina's Hill, go straight for the candy, steal it, and leave without us being able to do anything about it.

"Don't be scared. It could be that Panic is just telling a lie. Maybe we should plot revenge against Panic for accusing Pashelle like that."

Polo didn't know what to believe. I really didn't like the sound of his voice. It was quite hateful.

"What do you mean by plot revenge? What's that supposed to mean?" I said.

"We should do something to Panic to make him pay for accusing Pashelle."

"Like what do you mean?"

"We should stone him."

"Stone him?"

"Like what people used to do hundreds of years ago. Throw rocks at him. Or we should lock him up somewhere in a dungeon where no one can find him. And he won't be able to go trick-or-treating."

"Don't you think that we might get in trouble?"

"Not if no one finds out."

"How are we going to keep everyone from finding out? Dah … don't you think that Panic himself would know who locked him up or stuffed him in some kind of box?"

"Yeah, we could stuff him in a box. Lock him inside Pandora's box." Another suggestion from Polo. "We would blindfold him first. I mean, I don't know. Does anyone have any better ideas up their sleeves?"

Imaginations were certainly running wild now. I think that if we ever planned to steal our own candy, we'd fail miserably.

"The more reasonable thing to do is to get him to confess that he is lying about this. This way we don't get in trouble," Pannette said.

"How are we going to get him to confess?" I asked.

"We could threaten him. Tell him that if he doesn't confess, we'll beat him up."

That suggestion wasn't a bad idea, I thought. And it was possible. If we scared him enough, he might come out and tell the truth. Strange, though, that Pashelle hadn't mentioned any of this to us. Maybe she was avoiding the issue because she is guilty? Or maybe she was so innocent that to her, it was not even worth mentioning?

Either way, it served Pashelle right. She was always playing practical jokes on Panic.

One time she was in trouble for something else and had to help on vacuuming duty. She was vacuuming the main entrance area, and she had the vacuum still going accidentally on purpose just as Panic entered. And she directed the nose of the vacuum right at the doorway—right at Panic. Darn near sucked the seeds right out of his stomach, and she had the vacuum on full-blast too. She never misses an opportunity to get him. It's no wonder that Panic is stressed-out, worried, and paranoid all the time.

Not only has she been mean to Panic, she is always playing practical jokes on us. She has no shame. She doesn't think of the consequences of her actions. Making fun of our looks, our smarts, and everything. Sometimes she thinks she is so indestructible that it's as though she thinks she has steel armor around her. I couldn't help but think that she deserved this accusation, whether true or not.

"Maybe he's not trying to be mean. Maybe he is honestly mistaken and is simply wrong," I offered.

But that was irrelevant. We had to find out the truth. Was Panic playing a joke on Pashelle this time? The one thing we did know was that it would be no surprise if Wanda was hatching some kind of plan to steal our candy. It's expected every year.

"I'm not going to sit idly by and watch Panic accuse our friend like that. I don't know what to do right now, but something has to be done about this." The more we talked about it, the more upset Polo was getting.

Needless to say, this was disturbing news. We decided to wait for further information on this subject before we acted, and we decided to let this subject rest in the meantime.

The rest of the afternoon was spent doing nothing. No one wanted to play cards anymore. What was the point? No one would get satisfaction from beating Pashelle. Pannette decided to take a long bath. Pavneet was still sleeping, probably in complete paranoia, thinking she might not even wake up because of the pill she swallowed. Plato said that he was bored. It seemed like he was losing interest in our conversations more and more each day. From the expression on his face, it seemed like he was tiring of our idle chatter. Polo and Plato decided to go back to the Eye and play soccer. They had found out that Pele was going to be there that afternoon. Pele Pumpkin was an exceptional soccer player. I have heard some pumpkins say that he is so skilled, he could compete on the same playing level as people. That's quite the compliment. And I did nothing except watch the front door to see whether Pashelle would be released from the office and come back here.

An hour had passed. Pannette had soaked in her bath so long that she had become wet and heavy, and I had to help her out of the bathtub and onto the bed. And she used way too much bubble soap. She could hardly move. While she was trying to dry off, I did a pedicure and manicure on our nails. We wanted to look as nice as we could, right? No time to waste.

And then there was another knock on the door. This time I opened the door, and it was Papi. Or, I should say, Mr. Pumpkin. Our time had finally come.

"Are you ready to go?" he asked.

"You better believe it!"

Mr. Pumpkin picked me up off my feet and gave me a big hug. "How are you, Petrina? It's been such a long time since we last met. You must be excited."

Mr. Pumpkin is my favorite guard. Protector of the trees, as they are also called. His real name is Papi Pumpkin. He was a senior last year. As I mentioned earlier, a senior is someone who is in his or her final year of trick-or-treating. When a senior graduates, he or she becomes an elder. Only elders can refer to other pumpkins by their given names. All others would refer to an elder as Mr. or Ms. from that time onward. So I guess you could say his first year as "Mr. Pumpkin" was drawing to a close. It had been awkward calling him Mr. Pumpkin at first.

We were, and still are, great friends. He is well suited to be a guard, as he is very tall and strong and heavily built. It would be interesting to see if Polo was going to be as strong as Papi when he grew up. Papi won the arm-wrestling competition for the seventh consecutive time just a few weeks ago. That's phenomenal. I've always looked up to him, seeking his advice whenever possible. He is the closest thing I have to a mentor. Sometimes when I don't feel like walking, he carries me wherever I want to go. He has done anything and everything I have ever asked of him. Maybe I should ask him about Panic and Pashelle. Or maybe not. The truth is going to come out sooner or later, anyway. And there is nothing I can do about it.

"No kidding. Are you coming with us?" I asked him.

We could travel to the city on most days we wanted to, although there were limits on the number of times per month we could go. And when we did, we had to ensure that we were accompanied by a guard. We were too young to leave the Patch by ourselves. Too many bad things could happen to us in the city, the elders explain. So Papi, I mean Mr. Pumpkin, has accompanied me when I have traveled to the city.

"Yes, I am. But I will not be with you tomorrow. I have been assigned to be an extra guard in the Eye," he explained.

"Aw!" I exclaimed. "Why?"

I knew why, actually. He didn't need to answer. Extra protection in case of an attack from Wanda. Especially given the recent accusations.

"So who's coming now? Pannette, are you ready?" Papi asked.

"I'm ready." Pavneet had awakened and had gotten herself up off the couch. "Just give me a minute," she said as she went into the bathroom to wash her face and refresh herself. Even when she came out of the bathroom a few moments later, she still looked all groggy and half-asleep.

"Are you sure you want to come with us out into the cold city?" Pannette asked, thinking she could get Pavneet to change her mind and rest some more.

"You're one to talk," she countered, looking at the water all over the bed where Pannette was lying and probably thinking to herself that Pannette was having her own issues. "You're all wet. What happened to you? If you're going, then I'm going." We hoped it was said in a way that didn't set off any alarms bells for Papi.

The first thing we had to do when we returned to the Eye was to find out whether Pashelle was coming with us.

"Aren't you forgetting to bring something, Pannette?" I reminded her.

"Nope. I think I have everything."

"Are you sure?" I asked again, nodding toward the medicine bottle on the table next to her bed.

"Oh. Yes, of course. I almost forgot." She casually pretended to pick up something off the ground, creating a diversion, so she could grab the medicine bottle. She had taken it into the bathtub with her, attempting to determine what the pills were used for, but she still had no idea. I think Pannette has a desire to be a doctor or to work in the hospital in some capacity. That would be good. She could treat me if I ever become sick. Which is never, by the way. I am fit as a fiddle.

As soon as we started out toward the Eye, we were greeted by Pepper and Pickle. They were coming with us. They live between Pannette and Pavneet. They are having a birthday next week and will be turning six years old. I recall the birthday they had last year. We were invited. Do you know that neither of them eats cake? They didn't even taste their own birthday cake. They have never taken a liking to any sweet food. I think that is kind of strange. Like what pumpkin doesn't like to eat cake? Like what pumpkin is not going to eat his or her trick-or-treat candy? They are still going trick-or-treating, but they may not even eat any of it. How strange is that? Oh well, the more for the rest of us, I guess. I was most sociable to all the pumpkins that Papi had collected on the way to the Eye, greeting every pumpkin that I met, strangers and friends alike. As you know, I am very popular, and many pumpkins want to be my friend. But I only have so much time, do you know what I mean? I can't be everyone's friend, but I can certainly try my best.

We walked slowly toward the Eye, mainly because Pannette was too wet to move, and Pavneet looked like she was still sleeping.

"Maybe those were sleeping pills," I whispered in Pannette's ear.

Plus, Papi had to make a few more stops to collect more pumpkins for our trip into the city. As we tried to catch up on all the latest news and events from Papi, we admired the beautiful new shrubs and greenery that had been installed in this column. It's such a joy and instills a sense of pride in all of us. Our Patch must be one of the prettiest in the land, I thought to myself. That's probably one of the reasons why people want to come and visit us all the time.

 # CHAPTER 5
THE OFFICE

Once we entered the Eye through the West Gate, Pannette, Pavneet, and I veered left through the Rose Garden, while everyone else from our walking party went straight into the main entrance.

"We're not ready to leave yet, Mr. Pumpkin. We have some things we need to do first. Can you wait for us? We won't be very long. Can we come and find you in a short while?" asked Pannette.

Mr. Pumpkin said he would meet us near Halloween Headquarters, and we agreed.

"Can you do us a favor? Can you find Polo and Plato for us?" we asked Mr. Pumpkin. He said he would be on the lookout for them, and we made our way toward the office.

We walked westward, through the Rose Garden, which eventually turns into the Green Garden, which essentially is lush, green grass. There are no flowers in the Green Garden. After a short walk, we turned right, onto a path that leads directly to the office. We passed the hospital and the only garden in the Eye that actually has flowers during the fall and winter. This garden has the largest array of flowers in the Eye, such as mahonias, daphnes, and Christmas roses. The red river lily garden just outside the office entrance is one of the few gardens still completely full of flowers.

The office, hospital, and supply center are on the west side of the Eye, just north of the Water Gate. The office is actually right on the edge of Burnaby Bay, although you cannot see the water from anywhere in the building because of the Eyelashes. The office is a very old, almost ancient, four-story brick building. It was one of the few buildings not devastated by the War of the Broomsticks. It's a very spacious and roomy building. The third floor of the office is where the Elected Elders meet and make all the rules and decisions concerning the Patch. I have never been on this floor, so I can't describe it in detail for you. Suffice it to say that it has seats, benches, and tables conveniently located to allow for easy discussion on topics, ideas, and issues. That's what Mr. Pumpkin once said to me, when I asked him last year. The fourth floor is empty and is currently not used for anything. Not that I am aware of, anyway. I have not been on the fourth floor, either. Actually, no one is permitted to go to the third or fourth floor without the appropriate approval.

Pashelle would be on the second floor, which is the detention area. I have been on this floor, but only once. I have been in detention. Yes, this is true. I can say it again, if you want me to. I have been in detention. It was a silly incident that occurred earlier that year. I got mad at Ms. Pumpkin during class one day. She wanted to conduct an experiment. She needed everyone to be paired with another pumpkin. One of us had to close our eyes and fall backward and allow the other to catch us.

I got paired with Palmer Pumpkin, and I was the one who was supposed to fall backward. Well, I don't like him. It was supposed to be a game of trust, and I don't trust Palmer. Never have and never will. Not at all. So I wanted a new partner. There was no way he was going to catch me, and the chances were I was going to fall and land on my back. I could have been severely hurt. I could have hit the back of my head right on the hard ground, and I could have sustained a concussion or something. So I said no, that I wanted a new partner. Ms. Pumpkin said I had no choice. Like she was a dictator, if you know what I mean. And since I refused to fall backward into Palmer's arms, I got sent to the office.

I was told I had a negative attitude. Which to this day, I strongly deny. Like, don't we have the right to protect ourselves? What right does Ms. Pumpkin have to tell us to do something that would put us in danger? And I told her this, right to her face. But she didn't care. So I got sent to detention for the rest of that afternoon. I'm the most positive-minded pumpkin that I know. The whole incident was silly. It infuriates me every time I think of it. If I ever become a teacher when I grow up, I swear I will be the nicest teacher anyone has ever met.

The first floor is a wide-open, spacious lobby with a large atrium. As a prisoner on the second floor, the view of the atrium can be quite powerful and thought-provoking. There are paintings, sculptures, statues of famous pumpkins, and other types of art on the first floor. It's probably the cleanest area in the whole Patch. Not one speck of dust.

Pavneet, Pannette, and I went to the visitors' desk and asked if we could go to the second floor to visit Pashelle. Ms. Pumpkin told us to wait. She went up the stairs that kind of go around in a circle. She passed the second floor and continued up the stairs until she got to the third floor. We saw her proceed down a corridor, turn a corner, and disappear from view. The place was deserted. Like no one there at all. Luckily, we didn't have to wait long. Pashelle came down the stairs pretty much as soon as we sat down on a bench and got comfortable. She didn't seem stressed-out by her latest run-in with the Elected Elders.

"I'm free," she announced.

"You're so bad. What did you do?" I asked.

"Nothing. I swear on the very seed that gave me life. Honest."

"Are you okay?" Pannette seemed more sympathetic.

"I'm liberated, and I'm fine. They were asking me all kinds of questions. I got apple juice. And plus, I got to taste some freshly baked cookies from the kitchen. Ms. Pumpkin was trying a new recipe, and she brought some for the Elected Elders. And I was there. I had two cookies."

"They let you eat cookies while you were in detention?"

"I know, right?" Pashelle stole my expression. She can be such a copycat sometimes.

"Are you in trouble?"

"I didn't do anything wrong, so why would I be in trouble?"

"Did you tell Wanda about the candy?"

"Okay. So why would I do that, you idiots?" She didn't have to be so mean. We were only trying to help her. How could we help her if she was not being cooperative with us?

"Can you just tell us what happened, then?"

"The Elected Elders were asking me questions. They were boring questions. Who cares what they asked?" She sounded more defensive this time.

"We know that part. Why were they asking you questions in the first place, if you didn't say anything to Wanda? Why would Panic say those things?"

Pashelle hesitated for a second before speaking. "It was Panic? Oh, I am so mad. What a goof. I should have guessed. Who else would it be? That little rat fink. I'm going to stomp on his head and turn him into a squash."

I must interject at this moment and point out that squash are a different type of species than pumpkin. Although many people think that pumpkin and squash are related and that we come from the same seeds, we actually don't. As a matter of fact, we make fun of squash. How many squash does it take to make orange juice? Seven. One to squeeze the oranges, and six to hold the glass. Have you heard about the boy squash who played racquetball with a pumpkin? He got squashed! Aha. That was funny, wasn't it? Maybe not so funny.

There is a squash Patch to the west of Burrowsville, and we get together to have an annual golf match. Sometimes the golf team travels there, and other times the squash come here. Needless to say, we win every time. Squash are useless. You should talk to one of them, and you'd see what I mean.

Anyway, at this point I believed that Pashelle was telling the truth. Panic is a goof.

"So you're not getting a magical broomstick, then?" I asked, almost making fun of her predicament. "That's too bad. I was hoping you would take me for a ride somewhere."

"Very funny. I did talk to Wanda last night, though. Well, I'm not even sure if it was her or not. It was very foggy, and there were quite a few witches around. I was almost surrounded. Like I've never seen her up close before, right."

"Weren't you scared?"

"Like yeah. But when I realized she only wanted to talk, I calmed down a bit. She offered me something to drink. She said it was a concoction of bat whiskers mixed in with vampire blood."

"Did you have some?"

"Like gross! I can't believe you just said that."

"I thought you would have liked it," I said jokingly. "Mmmmmmm, how yummy," I said, licking my lips.

"Maybe if you drank it, you could have turned into a witch," Pannette added.

"Oh get out. That's so lame. Do you want me to tell you or not?"

"And this was last night?"

"Last night a few of us went to the city with elders to get more fireworks. They were afraid we might be short."

Fireworks are really important to us. The only way to prevent Wanda from flying over the trees and finding out about the location of the candy as it's being stored away, is to light fireworks in the sky. They make loud noises and create smoke, which deter her. All types of fireworks, like roman candles, skyrockets, torpedoes, flares, sparklers, firecrackers ... anything to keep Wanda and her loyal ghouls away from here. Who knows, maybe she would catch on fire or something.

Actually, the Elected Elders have been trying for years to have a retractable roof built over the Eye, similar to what people have in their sports stadiums. A roof that we could open and close any time we wanted. However, we don't have the physical skill set or the supplies to be able to do that. People would have to build the roof for us. And they have said many times that they will, but the end result is always the same. They say they don't have the budget to do something like that. Their Elected Elders, or government, argue among themselves about who should build it and who would do the work, and they can't agree, so it never gets done. They call it "bureaucratic red tape." Plus, they say that people will never get any benefit, so what would be the point? Needless to say, fireworks are essential for us. And they have become so popular during Halloween, even people use them now. None of us are exactly sure why they do. Just another thing they copy from us, I guess.

The more immediate question for me, then, became why Pashelle had gotten chosen for this task of going into the city and being a part of the fireworks group. Elders are supposed to choose the most behaved pumpkins for the fun volunteer jobs. That should have eliminated Pashelle from any consideration.

"My name got picked as a volunteer," she said proudly.

"You met Wanda Witch and didn't even bother to tell us?" Pannette was a little perturbed about that. I was angry at her because she got to go in the first place. Not that I was jealous or anything.

"It was all foggy, and I lost track of everyone. And then the next thing I know is there were all these witches surrounding me. They appeared out of nowhere. They were right in my face. They had me surrounded. I heard this really loud shriek. I think it was her laughing, but it was hard to tell. It almost broke my eardrums. She said, 'My name is Wanda Witch.'" Pashelle had temporarily changed the tone of her voice, to make it more eerie. And then she continued. "And I believed her. Although I never saw her. It was all dark, and there were too many witches laughing and screaming. And I yelled, 'Help! Help!' She told me to calm down, to have a drink, and that she needed my help. And moments later, the Five witches appeared."

The Five witches are opposed to Wanda's leadership. They were openly against Wanda taking control and have never taken the witch's oath under Wanda. Their names are Walda, Wera, Wila, Wyan, and Wyette.

Pashelle continued her story. "They told Wanda to let me go. They told me to run. And so I did. I ran. And you know what? I was running, and I saw Panic and I saw the elders, and I was safe. I just didn't want to think about it. Didn't want to remind myself. I never said one thing to her. And the next thing I know, I'm in here being called out because of stupid Panic!" Her voice was growing more enraged and louder with each word. Then she changed the subject, suddenly, almost as though she were tired of that nonsense.

"Is she sleeping?"

"Pavneet. Wake up. Wake up." I shook her until she awakened. "I think those were sleeping pills," I suggested.

"Those were sleeping pills? How did you find out?"

"We don't know. Maybe Pannette has some great ideas ... don't you?" I turned to look at Pannette, to see if she felt any shame yet.

"So where is Panic?" asked Pashelle.

"I don't know. Who cares?" I turned to face Pannette again. "So what are you going to do about the pills?"

"Me? Why do I have to put them back?"

"You're the one who stole them in the first place."

"Well, look at the bright side. She's getting her beauty sleep," Pashelle said.

We needed to come up with a plan to put the pills back before anyone found out they were missing. If Pannette had stolen them this morning, they might not have been reported missing yet. I would imagine the doctors and nurses do an inventory check, but how often? If we act now, we might be lucky. If we waited until the next day, that would set off alarm bells.

"Just throw them in the garbage. Or better yet, throw them off the cliff. How would anyone know that Pannette took them?"

She was referring to Petrina's Hill, I'm sure. In a way, that could be true. Did anyone see Pannette? I mean, the nurses would have known she was there, but did they actually see her take the pills? Were there any witnesses? Probably not. If there were, wouldn't Pannette have been in trouble already? So what were the options? Do nothing, or throw them in the garbage and hope no one found out it was Pannette. Option number three was to put them back. And option number four was to tell Dr. Pumpkin everything and then beg for mercy. If she did that, then how much trouble could she get into, anyway? She was only trying to help.

"Why don't we just tell Dr. Pumpkin?"

"No. Absolutely not. I don't think they would let me go out tomorrow. What if I can't go out? I could tell Dr. Pumpkin in a couple of days," Pannette suggested.

"Well … I don't know about that. Because they'll know those pills are missing, soon. Or worst case, tomorrow morning."

Pavneet had fallen back to sleep and was about to fall off the bench she was sitting on.

"Hold on, Pavneet. Keep yourself together. I got you. I think these are sleeping pills." I was almost certain.

"Oh hello, Ms. Pumpkin." It was Pinky Pumpkin, one of the Elected Elders. She was one of the few pumpkins lingering around the lobby. She had surprised us, suddenly appearing out of nowhere.

"Can I help you girls with something? Pashelle you don't need to stay here. If we have more questions, we'll call for you," she said.

"Okay. I know. We were just leaving."

"Is that Pavneet? Is she okay?" Ms. Pumpkin had noticed that Pavneet was hunched over, leaning on my left leg.

"Yes. She's fine. She's practicing for Halloween. She wants to be Sleeping Beauty."

What did Pashelle just say? Not very smart. Not very smart at all. Practicing to be Sleeping Beauty is not a smart thing to say.

"Okay," Ms. Pumpkin replied and walked away.

"Why did you have to say anything at all, you goof?"

"We're calling attention to ourselves. Look at those pumpkins up there." I nodded toward the second level. "They're staring. Come on, let's go. Someone take Pavneet's other arm."

"Who are they? Why are they in detention?" Pannette was trying to delay.

"That's Pie and Peyton."

"What did they do?"

"Peyton told me they were playing football, and he accidentally threw …"

"Who cares?" I interrupted. "Papi is waiting for us. We have to go. Like right now."

I received angry looks from both of them. They were probably wondering what my problem was. I can always tell what my friends are thinking.

"You take her home, Pashelle, while we figure out what to do with these pills. We'll meet you at headquarters." Then I turned my attention back to Pannette. "Let's go to the hospital. If the coast is clear, we'll try to put them back. If not, then we'll have to come up with another plan."

"Why don't you steal some waking-up pills while you're there?" Pashelle was making fun of us now. Even I had to laugh at that one, although I thought it was in poor taste, given the situation we were in.

CHAPTER 6
THE HOSPITAL

Pannette and I walked out of the office, through the red river lily garden, and stood behind some tall bushes at the side of the hospital, pondering our next move. Pashelle was half-dragging Pavneet, taking her home. The last thing I heard Pashelle say was how heavy Pavneet was.

"Okay, so now what?" Pannette asked.

"We'll need an excuse to go inside. We need to create some kind of diversion."

"Whatever we do, let's do it quickly. We have to go into the city soon. They're all waiting for us. It's going to get dark soon."

Just then, through the bushes, I noticed Peter coming out of the hospital entrance. What? What was he doing? Why was he in the hospital? Did he have some kind of a problem? Was he ill? He didn't know any of the doctors or nurses. Was he visiting? We stayed hidden in the bushes while we watched him walk right past us, hoping not to be noticed. We didn't want him asking unnecessary questions about why we were here. We watched as he walked slowly toward the Water Gate Bridge, where he met Prime, and they started talking. I wondered what they were talking about.

"Why is Peter talking to Prime?" I asked Pannette.

"How do I know? I'm not psychic."

Prime was good friends with Panic. We normally didn't associate with any of Panic's friends. He should have stayed away from them, as Panic and his band of goons are never up to any good. I hoped Peter was not in trouble. He was normally at home at this time. He didn't play sports very much, so there was no reason for him to be so near the soccer fields. Besides, he didn't spend nearly as much time at school as he should, so why was he in this area of the Eye at all? Maybe he lost something. I just hoped he wasn't in trouble with those guys. I hoped he hadn't done anything to them, causing them to be upset. He can get on pumpkins' nerves really quickly. I would have thought that if he had done something bad, he would come to me first. I'm the only one who has ever helped him. Was he asking Prime for help?

I turned my attention back to Pannette. "Well, what do you think?" I asked.

"I said I don't know. I have no idea why Peter is here."

"No. Forget about him. What do we do about the pills? Should we just go inside?"

"For what reason would we just go inside? We need a reason. Let's just forget about this and do something later."

"Like when later?"

Pannette didn't want to deal with this at all.

We searched the grounds and the entranceway to see if there were any guards around. After a long look, we concluded there was no one to be concerned about. I mean, mostly everyone was partying it up at the center anyway.

"How are we going to open the cabinet to put the bottle back inside, even if we get into one of those rooms? Wouldn't they all be locked? And how do we get into the same room? Wouldn't I have to put the bottle back exactly where it was?"

Pannette made some good points. The only way was for one of us to become injured in some way, which would give us an excuse to go near the medical rooms.

"Why don't I punch you in the face?"

Pannette was joking, I'm sure.

"I'm going to punch you in the face. No, seriously. I am," I replied.

I thought I should. And I should do it by surprise, so that Pannette didn't expect it coming. It might take the pain away. And serve her right in the first place. I decided this may be the best option, at this point. How else were we going to get inside? Yes, I'm going do it. I'm going to punch Pannette right on the nose. But I needed to catch her by surprise. I needed to wait for the right time. Not at this very second, because she was staring right at me, as if she were getting ready to punch me. She had this very manipulative look on her face. I needed to change the subject to distract her.

So I looked upward and noticed that the clouds were drifting this way from the north. The sky had been full of clouds all day. It was starting to get a bit chilly, too. And as I looked up into the sky, so did Pannette. So I cocked my right arm backward and brought my fist forward toward her face as quickly as I could. But because I wanted to catch her by surprise and because I was still looking up into the sky with her, I stumbled and lost my balance. And in self-preservation, I grabbed onto her, and with my weight moving forward, we both fell over right between the bushes, and I landed right on top of her. We didn't lie inside the prickly bushes for more than a second or so before she screamed, "Get off me!"

I'm certainly not going to take boxing as an elective at full-time school next year, that's for sure. We had fallen into a prickly bush, with thorns and very sharp, pointed leaves. And those bushes were wet. We were almost trapped inside, as if the bushes were holding us hostage. I wanted to get up off Pannette quickly, but in order to do so, I had to roll my body to the side, which meant I would land in a bush myself. Observing Pannette's facial expression, and seeing how much pain she was in, I wasn't sure if I wanted to do that. I wasn't being selfish. I just wanted to ensure that I didn't get any thorns stuck on my body also. To me, this seemed reasonable. It was a lot more comfortable lying on top of her.

So while she was still screaming into my ear—"Get off me!"—I ended up using her as a cushion, putting my hands and elbows on top of her chest, applying even more pressure, and pushing off against her to spring back onto my feet. It worked, but she became even more buried inside the bushes. She was stuck so deep inside that I couldn't even see her face anymore. She seemed satisfied, though, as she yelled, "Finally!"

She had more difficulties in getting back onto her feet than I did. She tried getting up but couldn't really move. She needed my help to get up. So I took hold of her hands and arms and attempted to pull her up onto her feet with one quick heave. I thought I was successful enough that she would regain her balance, and I let go off her. Lo and behold, she fell right back into the bushes again. She was obviously having balance issues. So I tried again. This time when she had her feet squarely on even ground, I hugged her tightly. And again we fell down, but this time she landed on top of me. Not in a bush, but on soft grass. She was heavy. It was my turn to scream, "Get off me!" When we could both stand up properly, I sighed heavily. We were both soaking wet. The dirty water smelled kind of gross. She stood motionless and was in pain. She was clutching her left shoulder. Pannette had thorns stuck into a good portion of the left side of her body. It wasn't pretty, that's for sure.

"You stupid idiot. I was just kidding. I wasn't going to punch you. Why did you do that? Ouch! Look at all these tiny prickles stuck on my body. My shoulder hurts," exclaimed Pannette.

I thought this was good. At least I had succeeded in finding a way for us to get into one of those medical rooms. I mean, sacrifices had to be made, right? I think it's referred to as collateral damage. We had no choice but to see a doctor right away, before Pannette's insides started coming out through the holes of her skin. We calmed ourselves and raced for the hospital entrance. Well, I tried to race, but she didn't want to. She walked very stiffly to the hospital entrance.

"Someone, please help us. Pannette has thorns," I yelled out to anyone who was listening as soon as we walked through the entrance. The nurse responded without delay.

"Pannette, it's you again. This is not your lucky day," said Nurse Pumpkin. "What happened to your shoulder? Are you in pain?" The nurse took hold of her right hand. "Let's go this way. No, not you, Petrina. You can wait here," as she put up her free hand to stop me.

I had to stop in my tracks. "Why do I have to wait here? She's my friend. I can help you. Do you need any help?"

"No, Petrina. We'll be fine by ourselves. You can wait here." She was rather stern and rude, if you ask me. Nurses are supposed to be comforting. That's what I was told, anyway.

"What happened to you?" I heard her ask, as she led Pannette down a corridor and into a medical room. I was forced to sit down in the waiting room. Well, this is just great. But at least we had made it this far. I wondered how long this was going to take. What was the nurse going to do, anyway? Was she going to pluck those sharp pins right out of her skin? Now that would be painful. It gave me goose bumps just thinking about it. I suffered a spasm and shook involuntarily. I had to take my mind off the incident. Besides, the smell in the hospital was annoying. It was weird. It didn't necessarily smell clean, though. The aroma was more like a very strong disinfectant. Kind of gross. I picked up a magazine from the nearby table and read the headline. It was a people sports magazine. The first page read, "Dallas Cowboys stay undefeated after convincing win." Wow. That's exciting.

Actually, I don't watch sports very much. But the photo of the players certainly told the story. People get so happy when they win at sports. Even pumpkins do. I was thinking of Parker when he won the individual golf tournament earlier in the summer. That win meant he was the team captain when they played the squash a few weeks later. He was really satisfied with himself. And Portia was so proud of him. She still talks about it, like it was yesterday. She talks about it as if she taught him how to play golf or something. Like yeah, right.

Pannette must have been gone for at least a half an hour. It took a long time. I hoped the treatment was all going well, and they were able to take all those thorns out. I was getting worried. I hope Papi hadn't left for the city yet. If they had already left without us, what would happen? Would we go later on, in the evening? How many more scheduled trips to the city would there be today? Would we have to go the next morning on an emergency trip instead to get our costumes? It was starting to get late. The sun was going down.

Pannette finally reappeared, with bandages over the front and back side of her left shoulder and other, smaller bandages down her left arm. My goodness that must have hurt. She must have been in pain.

"Well, things didn't go so well. The bottle of pills fell out of my sac," was the first thing she said after Ms. Pumpkin had left us alone.

"Aw!" I exclaimed.

"I have to meet with the Elected Elders tomorrow morning and explain how I got them," she said with a frustrated look on her face.

Now Pannette was in trouble.

"Not you now, too. Did you at least find out what type of pills they were?"

"They're sleeping pills. The nurse told me they're sleeping pills. I had to tell her that I had trouble sleeping, and needed help."

I knew it. I knew it. I knew those were sleeping pills. Didn't I tell you? I'm so smart. So on top of things.

"This whole thing is your fault. Why did we have to return the stupid bottle? Look at me. I have all these small holes over here," she said, patting down her left shoulder and left upper arm with her right hand. She seemed disappointed in me. Like I had given her bad advice.

"Don't blame this on me," I snapped back. "You stole those pills. You could have said you found them somewhere. You should take responsibility."

It was rare that Pannette and I argued, but we did. We had quite a heated exchange as we left the hospital. One would have thought that, since she was in pain, I would have had the better of her, but on the contrary. It seemed that the pain made her irritable and testy. We walked as quickly as possible back to the activity center, and after all that, we met everyone at headquarters. She called me a diva. Can you believe that? I am not a diva. I am many things, but I am not a diva. A diva, as I understand it, is someone who goes and seeks attention. Okay, I do not seek attention. As a matter of fact, I go out of my way to avoid attention. Like where did she even get that word from? Did she swallow a dictionary or something? Does she even know what a diva is?

As we approached headquarters, we decided to let it go and not let this predicament ruin our day. It was not as if a winner was going to be declared anyway, so what was the point? We both knew what the other had done. Neither of us felt the need to discuss it any further.

When we got to headquarters, would you believe there was Pavneet? Ready and waiting to get her costume!

"Did you take care of that issue? Did you find out what they were?" she blurted out aloud, as we approached the mass of pumpkins who were gathered there. Some of them gave us angry looks. Papi was not going to leave without us.

"I thought you were only going for a minute, but you two were gone for a very long time." Papi seemed a bit irritated himself. Before I had a chance to respond to either of them, questions were directed at us, about why and how Pannette ended up with bandages on the left side of her body. We had attracted a scene. It meant everyone within striking distance was staring right at her. Okay, so who's the diva now? I thought to myself. Isn't she the one getting all the attention at the moment? She's the diva.

Pannette was explaining to anyone within earshot that I had pushed her into a prickly bush—on purpose, I might add. She skipped over the part where she was at fault. Well, I guess she couldn't provide all the details. How convenient.

Pavneet was at least more subtle the next time and whispered in my ear, "Did you at least find out what those pills were?"

I ignored her question and asked my own. "Why are you here? You should be resting. Are you crazy?"

And she ignored mine. Tit for tat, I guess.

"It's last call for costumes. Anyone who needs a costume, we're leaving right now," announced Mr. Papi Pumpkin in a loud and clear voice. A few pumpkins let out a roar following the announcement. He collected his authorization papers and instructed us to follow him.

As we walked out of the activity center, I could hear a couple of pumpkins behind us snickering. I could hear them say things like, "Why did we have to wait for them?" and "We should have left them behind," and "We could be wearing our costumes by now." I felt like turning around and telling them to relax. Goodness gracious. Some pumpkins can be so impatient. I wanted to know who they were, so I pretended to turn around to look up at the sky to check on the weather, but I really wanted to catch a glimpse of their faces because I couldn't recognize their voices. And one of them was Palmer. He certainly has it out for me, doesn't he? Is he still upset with me about that trust experiment at school earlier this year? Like get over it already. I'm the one who spent time in detention. I was about to say something to him in my defense but decided not to. I didn't want to argue with him and give him the satisfaction.

Besides, it was costume time. We were going to the city. Now this was exciting!

CHAPTER 7
THE CITY

Over twenty of us still needed our costumes. We assembled, promised Mr. Pumpkin that we would behave, and began our journey into the city. Once Papi had organized his paperwork, he led us eastward through the gardens of the Eye. All my friends were with me. Peter and Porter also ran up to walk with us.

At the last minute, two of Pavneet's roommates also joined us. And they immediately ran up to the front of the group, where Mr. Pumpkin was. I heard one of them say something like "Where's my costume?" or "I can't find my costume" or "Someone stole my costume." And because of this, they had to come with us to get more costumes. Pavneet wanted to slow down. She didn't feel like having any conversation with Pansy or Panyin. So we let the other fourteen or so pumpkins race ahead, and we kept our distance a few meters behind them.

There are three main exits where we can leave the Patch to enter the city. The Farm Exit, which connects the farmlands to Burrowsville. This exit is near the greenhouse. The South Exit, which is accessed by walking down column CD03, which leads to New Surrey City. We would enter the city through this exit the next day.

And the East exit, better known as the East Gate, which also leads into New Surrey city. Today we would enter the city by leaving the Patch from the East Gate, which leads us to the city shopping center in downtown New Surrey City. The shopping center is similar to the Eye. The city has lots of stores and shops, with many choices of costumes, and downtown New Surrey City is the place to secure them.

Since our hearts were racing fast, we moved swiftly, and it didn't take us long to reach the end of the flat land. Even Pannette, wrapped up in bandages, was able to move quickly. Some of the pumpkins were even passing Mr. Pumpkin and had to be told to slow down. The East Gate is located just to the right of Petrina's hill. Instead of going up the hill to the left, we went downhill to the right. Papi led us through the tall bushes and then into a hole or tunnel inside the southern part of the hill. The East Gate is really an underground tunnel, which leads into the underground city subway or public transit system.

The tunnel is quite dark. There is no lighting inside this tunnel, so we had to watch our step. Some of us were given flashlights. Not sure why we all didn't get to carry a flashlight, but that's not for me to decide, I guess. I could certainly have used one, though. Peter had one in his possession. Not sure how that came about. It looked like six of the twenty or so pumpkins had flashlights.

Mr. Pumpkin ensured that he had enough rat poison in his possession to thwart any possible attacks by rats, mice, and other vermin in the tunnel. And the reason I mention the rats is because the strangest thing happened as we reached the end of the tunnel. Out of nowhere, we heard a pumpkin scream. We were alarmed, wondering what could have happened. Without delay, the pumpkins with the flashlights all pointed them in the same direction. It was Pansy. He was taken aback and was half hysterical. He was shaking. We saw a rat. "Use the poison, Mr. Pumpkin," we screamed collectively.

But Pansy himself took a can of spray out of his sac and starting spraying. Apparently a rat must have come down from the ceiling and hit him right on the head. He said he felt it. Eeewwww! How gross is that? I was quivering myself at the very thought of it. Well, he killed the rat by spraying it with the poison. He killed it pretty good, too. The rat had stiffened right up. Even the tail. The flashlights were pointed right at it.

I wondered where that rat came from. We're told that they are normally stationed on the ground. That the only thing we had to be careful of was not to step on one. So how did it hit Pansy in the head?

"How did that rat get so high and hit Pansy in the back of his head?" someone asked of no one in particular. Pannette and I looked at Pashelle to verify the look on her face and to see if we could determine any guilt. This was something she would do, no doubt. We all agreed it must have been a one-off incident and continued onward.

"Oh, poor Pansy. I should feel so sorry for him." It was Pavneet who whispered in my ear. I bet she got a kick out of that. Then, out of the corner of my eye, through the darkness, I noticed Peter and Pavneet nodding to each other. How strange was that? Looks like they were both amused by what had just occurred.

It took us twenty minutes to travel through the tunnel and to emerge on the other side. We arrived on the city subway platform, and we were greeted by the city guards or transit police, as they are better known. They ensure our safety on and near the subway platform. As we arrived on the platform, the two transit police officers blew their whistles and cleared a small lane for us to travel through. This area was very crowded with people.

The officers gave us a choice. Either they would escort us to the stairs that would lead us up onto the city streets or we could take an indoor flying machine, which is called an elevator. Some older and more experienced pumpkins can walk up stairs without much difficulty, but most of us in this group had very little experience going up giant stairs, so Mr. Pumpkin suggested we take the elevator. We all managed to fit inside. The door closed, we traveled upward, and within moments, the door opened, the officers wished us good luck, and we found ourselves on the city streets. Just like that. It's so simple yet so magical at the same time. Those police officers stay there twenty-four hours a day to ensure that no people or ghouls enter the tunnel. There is even a sign that says Pumpkins Only.

And the first thing you notice in the city is the number of people. It is crowded. The number of people on the city streets can be overwhelming. There are millions more people in the city than there are pumpkins in the Patch. There are probably more people on the subway platform on this night than there are pumpkins in the Patch. The comparison is not even close. I think it's important to note, though, that pumpkins are not going extinct as a species; rather, the city is getting overcrowded with people. Well, that's what we are told, anyway. Some elders say that it's a mathematical certainty that one day we will all run out of resources to make food because of the number of people. That one day there will not be enough resources to feed all the people in the land.

The second thing you notice right away is the speed at which people move. One can say this is so because their legs are longer than ours, but besides that, they move their legs purposely fast, as if every person is late for something, always trying to catch up with time. Due to these two things, we have to be careful not to be stepped on. I'm sure people would never do this on purpose, but accidents do happen. If you have ever seen pumpkins move within this mass crowd of people, then you would understand what I'm talking about. Some say it's inevitable.

I was told that Paloma Pumpkin died this way last year. She wasn't paying attention to where she was going and walked right in the path of a very large man wearing steel-toed boots. When he took a giant step forward, he ended up kicking Paloma right in the face. She probably had no idea what was going to happen until the very last second, when she saw the big boot come right at her, or surely she would have moved away. That must have been an ugly scene. Pumpkin insides were scattered all over the place. Her sister, Pelonia, watched the whole incident unfold right before her very eyes and was helpless to stop it. She was in trauma for weeks. She became so feeble, with no energy, that she was unable to feed herself. She lost all appetite for food. Eventually she just gave up on her life, as she had no desire to carry on without her sister. She was given as an offering.

Anyway. I'm getting off topic.

When people drive in their cars, they travel superfast. Uncatchable. The transit cars are even faster than the street cars. And overhead, you can see the airplanes, which are even faster than the transit cars. Although from the ground it looks like the airplanes are moving slowly, in reality they are flying. Literally. They move thousands of times faster than witches on their broomsticks. Again, the comparison is not even close. Mr. Pumpkin once said that an airplane could fly across the whole Patch in less than one second, if you can believe that. One second!

The city smells different than the Patch, too. The smoke and smog coming out of the cars and from the industrial buildings further east of the city is nauseating. The smell of the garbage lying on the streets is disgusting. In the Patch, the sweet scent of the flowers and the freshness of the trees, bushes, and other flora become obvious to the nose. I'm not the only one who says this. When people visit the Patch on tours, they say the same thing. That they wish their land smelled and looked as beautiful as the Patch. The gardeners do such a nice job of keeping the whole Patch clean and fresh. We often don't think about it in our day-to-day lives. But we are reminded of this when we visit the city.

This was actually only my fourth time in the city. The last time I visited the city, it was to visit New Surrey University or NSU, and we listened to a professor as part of a school field trip. He lectured us on weather patterns. It was an interesting topic, and the professor was nice to us, welcoming us into that lecture hall for that class. It was still difficult to focus because all the students kept staring at us. We can draw attention. Even though there are always pumpkins walking around in the city, and people are used to our presence, we can still be an amusement to them, with our short legs and bodies, our orange skin, and roundish shape. Actually I'm not in school quite yet. Next year will be my first in school. But we are required to take preschool lessons, where we learn the basics of pumpkin life, survival on the Patch, and the English language for a minimum of eight hours per week.

Speaking of the weather, it was cold. It was not raining, which was good. But the dark clouds overhead were still lingering. There were no pockets of blue sky at all. It looked like it was going to rain that night, and it might very well rain the next night as well. The forecast did not look good. I was keeping my fingers crossed, though.

After we came up from the subway elevator, we arrived on Ninth Avenue. We walked south along Ninth Avenue for about fifteen minutes, then turned left onto Cambie Street and walked another twenty minutes or so, until we came to a very large building, with many different types of shops inside. This building is called the Cambie Mall.

During our walk, many people we passed on the street welcomed us, saying and waving hello and good-bye. They always seem happy to see us. A few of them even stopped to ask us questions, but for the most part they tend to leave us alone. Of course, they knew that scores of pumpkins were entering the city that night and the next night for Halloween. People themselves participate in trick-or-treating, but they have only been celebrating Halloween for a short time. Some say the tradition of trick-or-treating started for them when poorer people asked the richer ones for food.

It's quite different for us, as there are no poor or rich pumpkins; we are all equal, and everything is shared. We don't trick-or-treat because we are hungry, per se. The common thought is that they copied the idea from us. That if the pumpkins can come into the city and ask for food, then why couldn't poorer people do the same thing? I mean, pumpkins have been celebrating Halloween for hundreds and hundreds of years, even before there were even people on the land. Well, that's what the elders explain to us, anyway.

As we neared the mall, I got a scare. Out of nowhere, a dog animal came rushing up to me, screaming "Woof! Woof!" Luckily for me, the dog was with a person, who was holding a rope tied to the dog's neck. That rope seemed to have stopped the dog because it looked like it was going to jump on me. It scared the living daylights out of me. And I am not even sure what the dog wanted. I couldn't even understand what it was trying to say. I don't think that pumpkins ever get to learn dog language, like people do. The person was nice, though. He said he was sorry. I think the dog should have said "Sorry," because he was the one who scared me.

The mall was full of pumpkins and younger people alike, getting their costumes on this day.

"That's it. That's the one I want."

Polo spotted his Superman costume as soon as we walked into the mall. The entrance doors were really cool too, by the way. They opened as soon as we got near them. Like they knew we were coming inside. I love the electrical gadgets that people use. The elevator ride was fun. I wish we had more of these amenities on the Patch. The only electrical entertainment we have is the giant television in the lounge. That's the one cool thing about the city. Lots of fun things to see and do. We see these gadgets all the time when we watch television, but to experience them firsthand is priceless.

Polo raced toward that store, went inside, and disappeared from sight. Mr. Pumpkin had the task of keeping track of where everyone was. Not sure how he was going to do that. Our group of twenty had scattered very quickly. The only thing Mr. Pumpkin wanted us to know was that we should meet back at this entrance in two hours. Pavneet, Pashelle, Pannette, and I entered the nearest store we came to. And it was crowded. The things in this store were amazing. There were all sorts of things associated with Halloween, like costumes, fireworks, lights, and decorations, and many other types of paraphernalia. We found the Pumpkin section, which had our shapes and sizes, at the back of the store.

"There aren't many choices in here … It's like all of the good ones are gone," I said, flipping through costumes that were hung on a rack.

We left that store and went into the next one. Same thing. The selection was quite limited. And that's how our afternoon went. In and out of as many stores as we could possibly visit. Peter, Porter, Polo, and Plato were also doing the same thing, trying to check out the costumes in as many stores as possible. We all were. Sometimes we found ourselves walking together.

"Hi Peter," I heard someone say, as she walked passed us, coming from the other direction.

"Who's that?" I asked Pannette. "Is that Peanut?"

She hesitated, squinted, and confirmed. "Yes. Oh, that's a really nice Snow White costume. That will look really cute on her."

Probably, I thought. I hadn't seen Peanut in quite some time and barely recognized her. Peter turned and started to walk with her and her friend Penny. I think it was Penny. They eventually entered a store that had ghost costumes. Well, good, I thought. At least someone is helping Peter with his costume because he needs all the help he can get.

Most of us had difficulties finding the right costume. Specifically, the right size. Pavneet found a beautiful princess costume, and I found the witch costume I wanted to wear in the sixth store we visited. The scariest-looking witch costume there was, with a really sharp-pointed hat. As soon as I tried it on, I knew. No questions asked.

"You're going to look scarier than Wanda," confirmed Pannette. We were having such a good time that we forgot all about the hospital incident from before. It was like it had never happened. Forgive and forget is our motto.

"Okay. I will wait in line. Someone go call Papi."

"Stop calling him Papi … It's Mr. Pumpkin, okay?" Pannette had to remind me again.

The purchase line was long. I had to start counting. Six people ahead of me. There should be a separate line up for us, don't you think? Aren't we special? I waited with Pavneet. Pashelle was trying on yet another costume, which didn't seem to fit her properly. Pannette went to go find Mr. Pumpkin.

The two girls in front of us turned around and started talking to us. They thought Pavneet's costume was pretty.

"Hello. That's so pretty."

"Oh. Thanks."

"And that hat looks really cool." It sounded like they were impressed with our choices.

I couldn't think of anything to say to them, so I just smiled. They said their names were Caillie Wilson and Makayla Webb. They seemed just as excited that it was Halloween as we were. And they were talking about all the things they had done and were going to do during Halloween. Which were about the same things as us. Isn't that funny that we actually had so many things in common? They did most of the talking. Pumpkins can be quite shy and intimidated when it comes to talking with people. Maybe it's because they are so tall and look so strong. They looked like giants, even though they were only ten years old. Did you know that some people can grow as tall as seven feet! Imagine that.

When it was our turn to purchase our costumes, Mr. Pumpkin still hadn't arrived. Pashelle had, though.

"Are you waiting?"

"Pannette went to go find Mr. Pumpkin."

We had to let other people pass us and make their purchases, even though we were really the next ones in line. We waited next to the line, near the checkout counter. And the people who passed us were so polite, asking, "Are you next?" and, "It's your turn now." A few more moments passed before Mr. Pumpkin finally arrived.

"Finally! What took you so long?" we teased him. We knew he had lots of pumpkins to tend to.

"Sorry, girls. I'm still trying to get organized, and I ..." He paused while he took out his paperwork. Actually, we don't make purchases with people money, per se. It's part of the unwritten agreement we have with people. Every year, Halloween supplies such as fireworks, costumes, decorations, and so on are given to us. Mr. Pumpkin is only required to fill out a form, and submit a voucher.

Mr. Pumpkin was probably running around the mall like a chicken with its head cut off.

I still wasn't finished, though, as I still needed to purchase various elements to put on my face, such as false teeth, some stitches, and maybe even some green coloring. And I needed a better sharper looking nose. I was told they were sold separately. I started to help Peter, who still hadn't found his ghost costume.

"Was that Peanut?" I asked him when she had finally left the mall.

"Yeah."

"What did she want?"

"She wanted to know why I wasn't going in the communal group," he replied.

If you ask me, I think Peanut should mind her own business.

"Like all ghost costumes are the same, Peter ... what's your problem?" I barked at him. I thought I might as well help him while I searched for my witch face elements.

It wasn't just Peter, though, who was having issues finding the right costume. Pashelle didn't find her "surprise" costume until the ninth store she visited. And the one she purchased looked the exact same one as three others she had seen two hours before. And by this time, it wasn't a surprise. She was Wonder Woman. No, I don't mean that she is a wonder woman but that she bought a costume that made her look like the character Wonder Woman.

No one seemed to mind, though, that it took Pashelle so long to decide because it just meant we stayed in the mall longer. And Mr. Pumpkin didn't seem to mind, either. This was the first year he was not going trick-or-treating. I wonder how that must have felt for him. It must have just felt nice for him to be a part of the process. We even stayed in the mall long enough to go to the food court. The food court was more crowded than the stores we visited. We sat down on chairs that were much too big for us. Well, in reality, the chairs were not big enough, because we could barely reach our arms to the table. I didn't need to use the table, though, as I only got a drink. I drank an orange and egg juice drink, called Orange Julius, which I like not just because of the color but because the drink is so creamy and soothing.

I was sitting next to a woman and a baby and another young girl. The baby was lying in a makeshift bed. He looked so cute. His face was so clean and without any facial hair. Most male people have facial hair. But he was so young that it hadn't had any time to grow on him yet. I tried not to stare at him, but I couldn't help myself. The elders say to never go out of your way to make contact with people. Don't talk to people unless it's an emergency. The older woman said hello to me and introduced me to the girl. The girl said her name was Victoria. The girl noticed me staring at the baby and said that I could touch him if I wanted to. Even though I was scared, I wanted to feel his skin. So I arose from my chair, got closer to the bed, and touched his hand. I think that was the first time I had touched a person. His hand was so soft. It was the size of my hand. Then the girl said I could talk to him if I wanted to, that his name was Alex. Well, I didn't know what to say to him. The baby was looking into my eyes, almost waiting for me to say something. I said '"Hello" and waited for a few seconds. But he didn't say anything back. So I said hello again. And still no response. I guess babies are like us … too shy to talk to another species.

Just then, Mr. Pumpkin got up from his seat and instructed everyone to get our things together. It was time to go home.

It was early evening by the time we left the mall. We were all tired. Shopping and visiting the city can be exhausting. But we all seemed to be satisfied at this point. Pannette found her Cinderella costume and her special shoes. There was really no point staying any longer. We left Cambie Mall in good spirits.

We started walking west on Cambie Street. We walked for about ten minutes. The streets were still full of many pumpkins. It was getting dark. Mr. Pumpkin reminded us that we should stay together. It was scary. The ghouls were flying overhead, some floating in the air, others hanging from the trees, making ridiculous sounds as if it were another language. It was difficult to tell who was who. Was that a ghost or a werewolf dressed up as a ghost? So confusing this time of year. The ghouls looked scary, though. It was a different feeling being up close to them. It was impossible for us not to notice them. They all seemed so close to us.

And then the strangest thing happened. As we crossed Sixth Street, Peter suddenly ran back east along Cambie. He took off. Along the way, he crossed a busy intersection and, my goodness, almost got hit by a car. What on earth was he doing?

"Peter!" we yelled.

Why was he running back toward the mall, all by himself like that? Mr. Pumpkin started running after him, and soon thereafter, we all followed. I was frantic with worry. It was one of the oddest things he had ever done. When he managed to cross the intersection, he finally stopped, picked up a broom, and held it up in the air. It belonged to a witch who came into view. The witch knelt down and grabbed hold of the broom and got on it. We could see from a distance that they were having a conversation. We were more cautious crossing the intersection and had to wait for the coast to clear before we proceeded. By the time we reached him, the witch had rejoined her friends up in the sky, and they all had flown away. We had assembled together on the sidewalk. Few people had even noticed what was going on. People lead busy and hectic lives.

"It was a witch. She fell," Peter started to explain before we had a chance to ask him.

"Peter, this is not acceptable behavior. Why did you run back and pick up that broom? Why did you talk to that ghoul? You can't do that."

"I know, right?" I added.

"Because I saw a witch fall, and her broomstick went its own way and landed here. And it looked like she was hurt. She hurt her leg."

"Peter. No!" yelled Mr. Pumpkin.

"Are you stupid or something?" I was not happy with what he had done at all.

But Peter was adamant about explaining himself.

"She hurt her leg and couldn't move. She fell down from the sky. And she couldn't move. And the people were not helping her. I saw one person even kick the broomstick farther away. I am almost certain she is one of the Five witches. They have never done anything bad to us. I wanted to help her."

All Mr. Pumpkin could think of to say was "No." Like no kidding. Peter is going to get in trouble. Big time.

"Peter you are never, ever to do this again. Running away from us. Running across the street with moving cars. That is as dangerous as it gets. Do you understand?" Mr. Pumpkin did not let up. He showed no mercy. I had known him all my life, and I had never seen him this mad and upset at anyone.

"But she needed our help, and I had to help. Because maybe one day, they will help us," Peter tried to reason.

I recalled a lesson that Ms. Pumpkin taught us in school earlier this year. She was talking about this thing called "karma." It means what goes around, comes around. This means that if you do something bad to someone, whether pumpkin, person, or ghoul, later something bad will happen to you. And the same thing the other way. A good deed will be returned with a good deed. I thought about the situation with Panic and Pashelle and how true that can be. Even still, Peter can be strange sometimes, you know?

"What did she say to you? We saw you talking to them before they flew away," I said to him.

"She said her name was Wera Witch. I said my name was Peter. And then they all said 'Thank you. You are very kind.' And I said, 'No worries.' And they left."

"Well, I think that is enough excitement for one day. Peter, we will need to talk to you at the office. As for everyone else, let's get back into an orderly line. Let's cross this road again and get home.

I think you all need some quiet time, so no noise on the way back. Forward march." Mr. Pumpkin seemed tired. It was a long day for him. Apparently, this was the third trip he had made escorting pumpkins to the mall that day.

Mr. Pumpkin was pretending to be some kind of general in an army. He is standing upright with his back straight. He was trying to be tough on us. But Mr. Pumpkin could never be tough on us. Papi had always had a light heart. I hope he is lenient when he explains the account to the Elected Elders. So up we walked again along Cambie Street. Surprisingly, Peter still seemed very proud of himself. He didn't show any remorse or guilt for his act of disobedience. In fact, he had a look of satisfaction on his face.

"Petrina, I want to go trick-or-treating in the communal group. I have already told Porter and Peanut that I will be joining them." He seemed to be begging me for my approval.

"No, Peter. You don't have to anymore. You're coming with us. I'm not talking about this again. Period." I had to be stern with him. He never listens to me. It can be so frustrating sometimes.

We continued our journey home. We all wanted to get there quickly. I wanted to try on my costume. We all did. Our trek would take longer than expected, however, because as soon as we turned back onto Ninth Avenue, up a few blocks, we were told that the road ahead was closed. Workers were fixing the sidewalk. There were pylons and barriers in the way, so we had to change our route and instead walk north along Eighth Avenue for a few blocks, then access Ninth Avenue just before we reached the subway. Well, this was an inconvenience.

"What's wrong with the sidewalk up ahead?" Mr. Pumpkin asked a person named Bob Lilly. He said the pipe underneath the sidewalk had burst and needed fixing, and it was not safe to walk past this area. Water was spraying up from underneath the ground, and it wouldn't take us very long to get back onto Ninth Avenue, if we took an alternative route. Well, like, hello. Doesn't he know it takes us longer to travel than people? Mr. Pumpkins' estimation had us walking at least an extra twenty minutes, if not more. And poor Pavneet, she looked exhausted. It was a good thing she sat down on a bench back at the mall whenever she had the chance so she could rest. So we took the alternative route. We had no choice. So from Ninth, we headed back east, and turned left onto Eighth Avenue.

Along Eighth Avenue, we had another scary moment. We had passed by a coffee shop, which was great. I love coffee. I wanted to go inside and buy some, but since we were running late, and since we had already had Orange Julius at the mall, my request was denied. Boo-hoo. But no big deal. I mean, generally speaking we're told to stay away from coffee houses because we can react badly to a certain aroma that comes from inside. And it's not the smell of the fresh coffee beans, either. There's a certain aroma that is so distinct to us that we naturally turn sour on it.

I'm not sure whether it was a pumpkin pie, or a pumpkin scone, or even a pumpkin spice latte, but the aroma coming from this coffee house was so strong, that Pavneet, being sick in the first place, threw up. Her seeds came out of her mouth so fast, it was like they were shot out of a cannon. I had never seen anyone throw up before. And she was standing right next to me. Luckily none of the seeds got on me. That would have been totally gross. My initial reaction was to get out of the way, from those missiles coming out of her mouth.

"Aw!" We let out a collective groan.

Mr. Pumpkin came to the rescue and tried to comfort Pavneet, putting his arms around her.

"That's okay, let it out, let it out. Don't be ashamed. You have nothing to be ashamed of."

It looked like she was about to throw up some more.

"It's the odor, it's the odor. Come on. Let's keep moving forward.

It's getting darker now," he said with a look of concern on his face, glancing up at the darkening sky.

I grabbed her costume bag, so she could travel light. Too bad Mr. Pumpkin hadn't brought any blankets with him, to keep Pavneet warm.

"Are you okay?" I asked.

Pavneet just nodded. She didn't look okay.

Not only was it dark, but it was starting to get foggy. I mean it was getting really foggy. It was so foggy that you couldn't even see the darkness. That doesn't make any sense, does it? Well, you know what I mean. But still no rain, and that was good news.

It was a long, slow walk back to the Patch. We went up Eighth Avenue, turned left on Oak Street, then right onto Ninth, left into the subway station. We made contact with the transit police, who escorted us down in the elevator to the underground subway platform. Then through the corridor that leads to the tunnel, which takes you back out at Petrina's Hill, out through the trees, and onto the east side of the Eye. Voilà … home sweet home.

We all were constantly looking at our costumes the whole way back. And I tried to keep Pavneet as close to me as possible.

By the time we had reached the Patch, it started to rain. Shoot. But only just a drizzle. Did I mention that I don't like the rain? It always amazes me, I thought, as I took one last look outside before heading into the activity center toward the dining hall, that when it rains, the fog lifts and goes away. Fog is really cloud and smoke. So that means water is stronger than smoke. I guess that's why water is thrown onto fire to put it out. Anyways, I think I'm just rambling on now because I'm so tired.

"I'm so tired," I said to anyone who was listening to me.

"I know, right," I heard someone say but was not quite sure who. There was a crowd of pumpkins all around me.

"I'm not going home. Let's just stay here. Besides it's dinner time. Look, there's already a line," Pannette noted.

My feet were aching, and my body was sore. I couldn't even begin to imagine how Pavneet felt.

"Pavneet, sit down here. We can get your dinner," Pannette said. We put all the costume bags down on a table, and we got in line. How many in front of us ... at least sixteen. Geez, why does it take pumpkins so long to put food on a tray? These lines take forever to move along. I wondered if it took people this long to put food on trays in their lineups.

"Thank you, Mr. Pumpkin, for taking us today." That was Peter. What a suck-up.

"You are very welcome, Peter. But we do need to talk tomorrow. We'll call you when we are ready."

Peter didn't seem too dejected or stressed-out about it, however. The look on his face was one of calmness.

"Hurry up, Portia. We're hungry too. You have enough food already. Are you feeding a cow or what?" Pashelle yelled. She was getting impatient. I hadn't the energy to yell that loud.

"Oh, that must be Pashelle back there. Relax, little girl. Looks like you have already eaten a cow." Portia Pumpkin was never one to take any sass from anyone.

"Don't get lippy with me," responded Pashelle.

"Oh. Shut up. Mind your own business. Wait your turn. Such a pushy one, aren't you?" Portia seemed to be looking for a fight with Pashelle. She even took a few steps toward us. And her friends Paris and Paige were ready to join in as well.

"You wanna go outside and fight it out?" Pashelle asked, as she was not one to back down, either.

"Hey. There isn't going to be any of that tonight," said Mr.

Pumpkin, who at first was going to let the argument go on but then decided against it.

It looked like for a second that Portia was going to take up Pashelle on her offer for a fight. Who has the energy for that today? Just come on and hurry up, and get this line moving. And it took quite a while. Portia and her friends seemed to take an extra longer time than usual, surveying the food choices before deciding to move on. Those three can be difficult and stuck-up at times. They are a few years older than us. They always think they can do better than anyone. Paige made it known to everyone that she was going to bring back the most candy. Big deal. Those three have to win at everything. Portia and Parker are quite an item in the Patch.

Parker is quite popular and very smart and may very well be an Elected Elder one day. There are some elders who are trying to groom him to be Elected Elder One. Even though he would only vote on issues if the other thirty Elected Elders could not decide, he would still have considerable influence and power. For example, if the issue was considered vital, he could cancel the vote and decide on the issue himself. The Elected Elder One is the highest-ranking pumpkin in the Patch. He is our leader. For your reference, the current Elected Elder One is Pudge Pumpkin. Furthermore, every pumpkin is allowed to call him by his given name. Meaning it's more than acceptable to call him Pudge. Anyway, Portia acts as if she is the one who made Parker smart. She acts as if he has her to thank for everything. Portia has a big ego. All three of them do. It's quite a mystery what Parker sees in Portia.

Once we finally did get our food and managed to find seats, we enjoyed chicken with fruit and salad, and I had apple juice to drink. We all ate quite quickly, since we were all hungry. Besides the Orange Julius at the mall, I hadn't eaten anything all day.

"Pavneet, are you okay? You are still so pale. You haven't said anything all day," asked Peter.

Is he still here with us? Why doesn't he go sit somewhere else? Does anyone really care what he thinks?

"I don't know. I'm just tired. I think the pill didn't help."

"The pill? The ..." Peter didn't finish his sentence.

Just then Ms. Pumpkin came by and offered her sympathies on the day's events.

"Mr. Pumpkin told me everything that happened today, Pavneet. Oh, you are such a sweet little girl. Don't be alarmed. You're not the first, nor the last, to have a negative reaction. You look so pale and shaken up by the whole incident. I think you should go home, drink lots of orange juice, and rest up. Tomorrow is going to be a big day," she said.

I think we're all going home.

We said good night to each other and decided to meet in the lounge first thing in the morning. Peter and I slowly walked home. I was so tired that I found myself walking slower than him, if you can believe that.

When I got home, I put my witch costume near the front door and then collapsed on my bed. I didn't wash my face or clean my teeth or anything.

Peter, on the other hand, put on his ghost costume and was playing with it. He was saying "boo" to himself. How lame.

As I got ready for bed, I started reflecting on all the things that had gone on that day. I hoped that Pavneet was going to be healthy enough to come the next day. If she got any sicker, she might not be able to. And not just because the elders said so; she might be too tired to go outside. She looked so pale all day—hardly any color on her skin. I actually couldn't believe that no elder had even noticed. Not even Papi.

But the elders had lots of things to do at this time of year. It was the busiest time of year for all of us, so who could possibly notice small details such as this. The cooks and kitchen staff were probably going to be busy all day preparing for the feast at night. There would be lots of food, and drinks, and deserts.

Extra security was implemented to ensure that everything and everyone was safe. Especially now with the rumor that Pashelle told Wanda Witch where the candy would be stored this year. Who knew if that was even true? What type of punishment, if any, would she receive? Would she be allowed to come tomorrow? Maybe I should talk to Panic in the morning and see if I could get the truth out of him. I needed a plan of action.

And my Lord, why did Pannette have to steal that medicine from the hospital. How much trouble was she in?

Can you believe that my three best friends were all in trouble in some way and might not be able to come with me on Halloween? This was so absurd, it was laughable. A day we had been waiting and thinking about forever was finally here, and we might not be able to go trick-or-treating together? Too many things to think about.

Well, how long was it that I had been lying there? I thought I was tired and sleepy. If so, why hadn't I fallen asleep? I was starting to think there must be some magic trick to sleeping. I should have kept one of those pills for myself. Peter played with his ghost costume for a bit, then lay in bed, and now he was out like a candle. And I was supertired, just lying there thinking about the day. Should I try counting sheep again?

What was that noise? Was that a werewolf howling at the moon? Didn't sound like a witch … That was a really loud noise.

So here we go with the sheep. One … two … three …

And why was Peter talking with Prime earlier today? Like what was that all about? What was he doing in the hospital? Maybe I should ask him. But then he would know that I had been there. I didn't want him to find out I was there or set off any alarm bells. Why would he even associate with one of Panic's friends? Those two, plus Plunder and Perses, have given him such a difficult time since the day they were born that it's unbelievable he would even talk with any of them. They are such bullies to him. He needs to start standing up for himself and protecting himself. Or maybe they weren't bullying him, and Peter really was friends with them. Was that possible? Was Peter friends with them more than us? Oh my God, this is almost embarrassing. Did he not have any sense of loyalty at all? What was he thinking? I know he was desperate to find friends, but I think that kind of crossed the line a little bit. And running across a dangerous road, just to help those witches.

Oh, he was lying right on top of his glasses. I should have moved them away from him so they didn't break. But I was too tired to move. Too tired to move and too tired to fall asleep, but not too tired to think about the adventure that awaited us the next day.

Sleep ... sleep ... sleep ...

# CHAPTER 8
HALLOWEEN

What time was it? It was already eleven. I must have slept in. I cannot believe I slept right through the morning again. I need to start sleeping sooner, so I can wake up on time and start eating breakfast. Oh well. But for some reason, I didn't feel like having my morning coffee. I wonder why that is.

It looked like Peter had already left.

Well, this was it. It was finally here. It was Halloween. This was the moment I had been waiting for all my life. This was exciting!

I washed my face and had a quick bath. I got myself ready as quickly as I could. I quickly tied my blue bow on my stem.

I looked out the window and checked the weather. It seemed cold, dark, gray, and windy. Even though the clouds were dark, thick, and scary, however, it appeared it was only raining ever so slightly. Let's call it a drizzle. The clouds were moving quite rapidly across the sky, though, as if they were late for an appointment. I prefer clouds that are relaxed and take their time. Lazy clouds. Pannette and Pashelle must already have been at the Eye. But I wasn't sure about Pavneet.

As soon as I left the house, I met sisters Penelope and Piper, with their friend Pauline. Those three are my neighbors to the south. We walked together to the Eye. They are three of the most well-groomed and neatest pumpkins we will ever come across. They probably have two baths in the morning and maybe two at night as well. They are quite chatty. They are three years older than I am. This will be their fourth year of trick-or-treating. It's difficult to get in a word with them.

They spent most of the trip talking about school and the assignments they had to complete. Apparently, Penelope hadn't finished hers and wasn't sure if she was going to finish before the due date because of Halloween. In preschool, we don't really get any take-home assignments.

Trips to the Eye seem to go faster when I walk with them. They are a terrific source of knowledge for me about what to expect in the coming years. Not just about school, but about everything. They told me that I would love trick-or-treating. Like, I know already.

When we passed through the West Gate, I noticed that many pumpkins had gathered to the right, in the Lily Garden. It seemed like a different type of commotion than usual. I wondered what was going on, It seemed like they were watching something interesting. Actually, there was a crowd of pumpkins all over the Eye Gardens. There was a traffic jam. It's funny how I never noticed this many pumpkins last year or the year before. I let Penelope, Pauline, and Piper go through the Rose Garden, and I turned and joined the melee in the Lily garden.

"What's going on?" I asked a stranger. I had seen this pumpkin before but couldn't quite recall his name.

"I think there's going to be a fight," he replied.

"What? Who?" I asked.

"I can only see Panic and Plunder," he said, pointing toward the big tree in the middle of the garden.

"Who are they fighting with?"

I didn't wait for his answer but instead tried to push my way through the pack until I could get a clear view of the action. Not because I wanted to see a fight but more out of curiosity. I wanted to know who they were. And when I got closer to the tree, I saw Polo and Plato. And they were in Panic's face. I mean, right in his face. Panic was being pushed back against a tree. Oh my goodness, are they are going to fight?

Some of the pumpkins were even encouraging them, yelling "Fight! Fight!" This was vulgar. Interesting and exciting, but vulgar.

Just as I was about to scream, "Polo ... no!" some elders noticed the noise and commotion as well. They came rushing out of the activity center and were running this way. They were pushing through the crowd, yelling, "Break it up! Break it up!" as if they knew a crowd like this could cause a riot. I am sure they have experience in dealing with this type of thing and could sense what might result. I did not see any punches being thrown in either direction. But I had just arrived, and could hardly see through the crowd.

"Everyone back away. What's happening here?" It was Mr. Pumpkin. Now he's one of the most popular pumpkins on the Patch. He is an Elected Elder, and many think he would be an ideal candidate to be Elected Elder One, one day. Mr. Pumpkin can be very excitable and funny at times. Although it's rumored he has little interest in the general activities of the Patch. Most pumpkins respond to his leadership style. He's very chubby, as he spends much of his day eating and drinking in the dining hall. His given name is Percival.

"Calm down. Calm down." He was speaking loudly so everyone could hear him. He has a recognizable and distinct voice. And he certainly has a lot of air in his lungs, which allows his words to come across clearly. "Everyone just calm down, calm down. Okay. Calm down."

It was quite odd because, although he was the one instructing everyone to calm down, it was he, himself, who was getting hysterical. He was accompanied by two other elders, and the three of them were separating everyone. Pumpkins had no choice but to make room and let them through.

Polo and Plato were being pulled away, as the elders got between them and Panic. And pretty soon, all of them were walking westward, most likely to the office. Polo was still yelling at Panic as they passed by me. He was saying things that were quite crude. I was kind of surprised. I had never heard Polo say such vulgar words before. He was really upset with Panic. I had never seen this side of him. He was probably just trying to be protective of Pashelle, I guess. And for Plato to be involved in something like this? Wow. Plato Pumpkin is the philosopher type, not a brawler. Plato is always calculating the odds of success or failure, always looking for a logical solution to a problem. I wouldn't have thought he would conclude that pounding in Panic's face was the right thing to do.

I started to walk behind them, in the same direction, trying to hear more of the conversation, but there were too many pumpkins in the way. I could never get close enough to Polo or Plato to ask them what happened. It didn't appear that any punches had been thrown in the melee. Well, I hadn't seen any. There went my chance to talk to Panic.

There was still a lot of whispering and dialogue among pumpkins, even after Polo, Plato, Panic, and Plunder had disappeared from sight.

"I think Polo was going to punch Panic," I heard someone say.

Great. What a lovely start to the day.

"Why?" inquired the other pumpkin.

"Didn't you hear what Panic said this time?"

I wondered what Panic had said this time. He must have said something to Polo to ignite him like that. Oh, who cares? I tried to tune those two strangers out. I didn't want to hear any more rumors. I was much more interested in the truth. What could these strangers possibly know, anyway?

Panic was certainly not the most popular pumpkin in the Patch, that's for sure. He could be dishonest at times. It was interesting to note, from listening to the chatter this morning, how few pumpkins knew about the rumor of Panic and Pashelle. I would have thought this was common knowledge. I guess the elders had done a good job of keeping a tight lid on the incident.

I should have shaken some sense into Polo and Plato the day before—before they tried to do something stupid. This kept getting worse. Now they were in trouble. What if they couldn't go out that night? I was running out of friends to go trick-or-treating with. I must admit, I was starting to feel a little desperate.

"Okay, Petrina, just relax," I had to tell myself. "Let's see if we can find Pannette." I passed through the Lily Garden, then through the Rose Garden, and neared the activity center. Wow, it was abuzz with commotion. I looked around, but I didn't see any of my friends at first glance. But it was hard to tell. Many pumpkins came to the Eye this morning already dressed up in their Halloween costumes. So it was difficult to tell who was who.

Peter snuck up behind me. "Hey. How's it going?"

"Why is your costume so big?" Peter was wearing his costume, although we weren't leaving the Patch for hours yet.

"Didn't you try it on before you got it? Oh no!" I suddenly realized I had left my costume at home. It was still near the door. "I forgot to bring my costume with me. It's still by the door. Can you believe that? What a goof I am. Now I have to go back home."

"Oh. It's not that big. Just a little loose. Hey?"

He was about to say something but hesitated. He was almost waiting to get my attention again.

"Yes … what?" I said after a lengthy delay, encouraging him to say something.

"Porter and Peanut asked me about the communal group again. And a few other pumpkins asked if …"

"Peter, do we really have to go into this yet again? Did you go to the office and meet with the Elders?"

I thought for a minute that, with all my friends potentially in trouble, the only pumpkin I might end up going trick-or-treating with was Peter. Oh, this was a disaster waiting to happen. This was depressing. And Peter was trying to make things even more difficult.

"Yes. Everything is okay. I explained why I did what I did. Do you know why … because I was talking to …"

Just then I spotted Pannette in the crowd. "Pannette. Pannette. Over here. Where are you going?" I had to scream it out.

"I will talk to you in a minute. I have to go meet with the Elected Elders first," she yelled back, as she came out the main entrance.

I felt like advising her to tell the truth, but she had already confessed to the whole incident. Well, I think she had, anyway. Pashelle had found me and began pushing pumpkins out of the way to reach me.

"Did you see what happened outside, just now?" I asked.

"No," she replied but then turned her attention to Peter. "Hey, Peter. Isn't your costume a bit too loose?"

She's always bullying him. I felt like putting Pashelle in her place, once and for all. But I would have been defending Peter, at the risk of losing Pashelle's trust. She can be blunt and straightforward. But the one thing I know about her is she would always have my back. She would always come to my rescue if I was in trouble. That type of friendship can't be replaced. That type of friendship is priceless.

"Polo, Plato, Panic, and Plunder almost got into a fight."

"No way … and I missed it?" That was Pashelle's thing. She can be quite aggressive and loves confrontation. Whether she is in the middle of it or not. "Where are they?"

"They got taken away to the office."

"What do you mean? Did you see them fight? Like they threw punches at each other?" I could tell by the look on her face she was disappointed she had missed the action.

"No. Well, I don't know."

She turned to Peter.

"Did you see what happened?"

I didn't let him respond. I wanted to know whether or not Pashelle was still in trouble.

"So what's happening with you? Have they asked you more questions?"

"'Who?"

"The Elected Elders. Did they call you back into the office for more questioning?"

"Nothing happened, Petrina. Read my lips. Nothing happ—"

"Okay. I know what you said."

"They can't prove anything. And do you know why they can't prove anything, Petrina? Because I didn't do anything. You look so worried."

"Well ... I am a bit worried. Speaking of worry ... have you seen Pavneet?"

"I don't know. I just got here. She could be at home still. I was just talking to Ms. Pumpkin, and she was telling me that it can be a traumatic experience to realize people eat pumpkin. I'm like, I know, right. Doesn't help she may have swallowed sleeping pills," she said, as if it were my fault.

"Hah, hah. Very funny. She didn't see them eat pumpkin. It must have been the smell. It can be quite strong, can't it?" Pashelle nodded in agreement. "Come on, we should go eat or do something."

We weaved our way through the crowd and made our way through the main entrance and then into the dining hall to see what type of food there was for lunch. We left Peter behind to do his own thing. It was a party-like atmosphere. Heck, what am I saying … it was a party. It seemed like the whole pumpkin population was there. Some were singing to music and dancing. Others were playing games.

"What's the point? There's no way we're going to find a seat."

"I know, right."

I wished she would stop saying that.

"Besides, I'm not hungry, anyway."

Peter was not the only one wearing his costume. Not only did Preston have his Dracula costume on; he told me he had worn it to bed the night before. And it looked like it because it was all wrinkled. Pretty was wearing the most beautiful Goldilocks costume. Petal was dressed as a baseball player. Pan was dressed as Buzz Lightyear, a character from the movie Toy Story. Pashelle said Parker was dressing up as a guitar, and Portia was going to be a rock singer. I wondered whether Paige and Paris were going to round out the ensemble by being drums and a piano or something. Pamper was dressing up as a big giant baby diaper. Wouldn't want to be near him if an accident happened. Where had they gotten these costumes from? The older pumpkins had the more original costumes. By comparison, ours were actually quite basic. I guess this is the difference between the first years and the older ones. Mine was still scary, but simple. Even the elders had costumes on. Mr. Pumpkin was dressed up as Mohandas Gandhi, complete with clean white sheets and a cane. Ms. Pumpkin was an angel, with a halo that was brighter than the sun.

"Pashelle, I have to go home and get my costume. And I might as well go see how Pavneet is doing." I didn't want to stay in this mass crowd, anyway, even though the aroma from the kitchen and dining hall was amazing.

"Okay, sure. I'll wait for Pannette. She had to go to the office and talk about how she got the pills. We'll come over as soon as we can. If I see Polo and Plato, I will tell them where we'll be."

So off I went back home. I left the Eye in its euphoric state. It was so loud in the center that I couldn't even hear myself think. But as I was going home, all I could think about was coming back to the Eye as quickly as I could. I found myself walking really fast. Running, almost. On the way home, I ran into two friends whose names I couldn't remember. I see them walking along column RY07 all the time. They live four houses south from me. They were dressed up as Bert and Ernie, characters from the show Sesame Street. They always seem so amazed to see me. They whisper in each other's ears, "That's Petrina," each time they see me, but they never actually say hello. It makes me feel like I'm famous or something. Like they know me, but I haven't given them permission to say anything. I always smile back at them, pretending they have said hello.

As I approached my house, I did greet Mr. Pumpkin, who was pacing up and down the column, performing his duty. He must have a difficult job. It must be kind of lonely. He just walks up and down column RY07, pretty much all day. His job is to guard this column. I should talk to him more often, but he is so much older than I am. Like he is really old. We have nothing in common, so it's hard to say anything except hello.

I grabbed my costume, decided to put it on, and made my way to see Pavneet. I didn't put on any of the face elements, though. I kept those in the store bag. When I arrived at Pavneet's, she was awake. This was a good sign.

"Hey there." I greeted her with a big smile. "How are you feeling? Is anyone home?" This is something we always have to ask before entering. Because if any one of her roommates are home, there is no point in coming inside. Her roommates don't like Pavneet to have any visitors.

"Yes. Feeling much better. So far, anyway." Then she changed the subject. "Well, look at you. That hat is really tall."

I went to her bedroom and looked at myself in the mirror properly for the first time.

"Aren't you going to put these things on?"

"Should I? I guess I could. Maybe I should at least put on the green paint."

"Yeah. Let's do it. I'll help you. Then you can help with this." She took her princess costume out of the bag and held it up to cover her body. I looked at her in the mirror, and she looked pretty.

While we got ready, I was telling her what a riot it was in the Eye. Literally.

After we applied my green paint, I helped her with her costume. She looked like a doll. So cute.

"You are the prettiest pumpkin in the land, Pavneet," I said. And she told me I was the scariest witch she had ever seen. I put the fake, sharp-pointed teeth in my mouth and made a sound resembling that of a witch.

"Are we ready to go?"

"For sure."

Poor Pavneet. She is the most talkative person I know, and this sickness had taken all her energy. What a time to get sick. The worst time.

So we slowly made our way back to the Eye. We normally talk about everything and anything, but not today. We talked very little. Actually we talked about Peter, of all things. He had come to see her earlier in the day to check up on her. Apparently, Peter and Pavneet were very close. I hadn't realized. She was telling me how she thought Peter was funny. I was like, what? He is the most boring, dull, and uninteresting pumpkin you will ever meet. Peter had told her all the things that were going on, and the excitement in every pumpkin's eyes. And how he had met with the Elected Elders.

Apparently, Peter had come to visit her a few days ago and had almost gotten into a fight with one of her roommates. Like, really?

"This was just a few days ago. He was with me when I first got ..." and she stopped her sentence midway.

"When what?"

"When ... oh, never mind." She did not want to complete her sentence and instead started a new one. "Wow! Look at everyone," she said as we neared the West Gate.

Just in the short time I had been away from the Eye, it seemed like the traffic had doubled. And I thought there were lots of pumpkins here this morning.

"It's funny, Petrina. I don't remember this much excitement here last year. I remember, but I don't really remember ... Do you know what I mean?"

She took the words right out of my mouth.

As we neared the main entrance, we could see that barriers and pylons had been placed strategically in the Eye to assist us with direction when we all left the Eye later. There were also informational signs attached to posts, with big orange arrows pointing in various directions. The guards in the Eye were stationed accordingly, as if some of the first trick-or-treaters were preparing to leave. I was getting goose bumps. Like, seriously. I had butterflies in my stomach.

We entered the center and pushed our way to the back of the building, toward the lounge. This is where we try to meet up every morning. It's a social place. There is a big television that's always on, showing events from around the land, outside the Patch. You can get alcoholic drinks here, but not us. We're too young. You have to be an elder. Yet another benefit of becoming a Mr. or Ms. Pumpkin.

And it's crowded in here too. I wondered if we wanted to stand if we couldn't find any seats.

"Do you want to stand here if we can't sit down?" I asked Pavneet.

"I don't know. I guess. Where else are we going to go? This is like a pumpkin traffic jam. We're packed in like sardines in here," she replied.

"We could go back outside. At least we can get some air," I suggested.

"Maybe. It's starting to get really sticky and sweaty."

"It reeks. It smells kind of gross."

"Maybe big baby diaper finally exploded," she said, laughing at her own joke. Peter must have told her about Pamper.

"Yeah, okay. Let's go back outside."

So we forced our way through the crowd and went back out the main entrance. Still no sign of any of my other friends. Oh, but wait. Didn't I tell Pashelle that we would meet her at Pavneet's? No, I said we would meet at Pannette's. No, wait. I think I told her we would meet in the lounge. Should we just walk back to Pavneet's, I wondered. I suggested that we walk back.

"Wouldn't we have seen them on the way here?" Pavneet wondered.

"Unless they left just as we got here. And we didn't notice because there are like a million pumpkins all over the place."

"Should we go back?" Pavneet asked. "I don't want to walk all the way back home."

"We should just stay here because this is where we have to be anyway. Right? They'll come back."

"Pashelle is going to punch you in the face," Pavneet warned me. And she was probably right. If I messed up our meeting place, Pashelle would be mad.

We waited about twenty minutes, staring at all the pumpkins gathered in the Rose Garden, before Pannette found us.

"Hello. Good morning. And isn't it a really, really, really, really good morning?"

"Okay. We know," said Pavneet, interrupting Pannette.

"Well?"

Pannette's faced turned a bit sour.

"Oh geez."

"What happened?" Pavneet inquired.

"Pannette met with the Elected Elders this morning," I told her.

"And ..." I turned to Pannette.

"I have to do twenty hours of community service in the hospital."

"Aw! Okay. But you're coming tonight, right?" I wanted to keep her focused on the real priority. "Hey, where's Pashelle? Isn't she with you?"

"Like, didn't you hear what I said? Twenty hours. One hour per day, or four weeks.

"No, three weeks," I corrected her.

"No. That's four weeks."

I wondered if I should make another attempt to correct her.

"It's three. It's actually less than three."

She gave me one of her angry looks. "Like, you can do math, right?"

I didn't think that was really a question. Yeah, okay right. That's four weeks. Wasn't she counting weekends? Who cared? At least it wasn't me.

"Okay. Yeah, right. But everything is good for today, right?"

She nodded. Good. Everything seemed to be falling into place. Everyone seemed to be avoiding any discipline today. Disaster could be averted, after all.

"You look scary. I really like the green paint. You look like the Wicked Witch of the East." Pannette liked watching television.

"Oh … like from the yellow brick road movie?"

"I think it's called the Wizard of Oz," Pavneet corrected me.

We waited, standing right in the middle of the steps that lead up to the main entrance. We had a bad habit of doing that. We would watch everyone come in and out. But today it was starting to get annoying. This seemed like the busiest spot in the whole Eye. Perses, one of Panic's friends, walked up the steps, veered to the left, and bumped into Pannette, accidentally on purpose. His shoulder hit Pannette right in the back, knocking her off balance. What a goof Perses is, I thought. Pannette winced in pain for a brief second, flexed her left shoulder, and turned around. But she didn't notice who it was, thinking the incident was due to traffic and congestion.

"Why are we standing here?" Pannette was starting to have doubts that this was the best spot to hang out that day.

"Trust us, it's not any better anywhere else," Pavneet told her.

"Don't you think we should move away and sit somewhere in the garden?" Pannette suggested. "Or let's go to the lounge."

"Yeah, okay, Pannette, let's go outside," I said, as if she had just come up with this brilliant idea.

As soon as we found ourselves in the middle of the Rose Garden, Pashelle spotted us. And she raced up to me and gave me a push. I mean it was kind of a strong push that knocked me off balance.

"You stupid goof," she said angrily. "Why are you here? You said Pavneet's."

I was about to apologize but thought to myself, What's the big deal? So she got some exercise.

"What's the big deal?" I said.

"I walked all the way over there for no reason."

"It's called exercise, Pashelle."

"You're the one who needs exercise. Don't give me that excuse."

I started laughing. "I'm not laughing. I'm sorry. I got confused," I said, feeling just a tad guilty.

"Okay, so what do we do now?"

"Wait, I guess."

"Let's wait inside. It's getting a little windy out here," said Pashelle, as if she had just come up with this brilliant idea. We don't always think alike.

"There's no room to move inside. We were in there, and now we're out here."

"Let's just wait here. The ceremony must be starting soon," Pannette said.

She was referring to the opening ceremony.

And wait we did. We moved toward some empty benches in the Rose Garden and sat down. We talked about the messages on the boards and admired the fancy arrows on the sign posts. We talked about how weird we looked dressed up in our costumes, as we sat, hunched over on the benches in the Rose Garden, paying attention to the movement and whereabouts of all the pumpkins.

"You look so pretty. We should dress up like this all the time."

"Put on your crown."

"It's called a tiara."

"A what?"

"Tiara. If you are a princess or queen or something, this is called a tiara."

"Same thing. Just put it on. Let's see."

Pavneet put on her tiara. She will find her prince one day. No doubt about that.

"We still need to get our pictures taken. Why don't we do that?"

"Because there's probably a million pumpkins there right now."

"No. Ms. Pumpkin said that you take your pictures when you sign out, at headquarters."

"Oh. Well, that makes sense."

"Like you passed the test, right?"

"Do you think you could leap a tall building?"

"Why? Like how could I do that?"

"Just answer. Just play along."

"I am playing along. Superman leaps tall buildings, not Wonder Woman."

"What does she do?"

"She's a female superhero. These bracelets do things. They are called Bracelets of Submission. They defend her. She's supposed to be really fast and have superreflexes and be a really good fighter. And this tiara acts like a weapon."

"Has anyone seen Plato or Polo?"

"Where's Peter? He's coming with us, right?"

"Did you see Pita?"

"Peter is here somewhere."

"No. Pita. She's dressed up like a sandwich. She looks like a vegetarian wrap."

"Didn't you see any meat on her? How do you know she's vegetarian?"

"I don't know. I've never seen her eat meat."

"Oh. Look at those two … near the trees."

"What are they supposed to be?"

"Who knows? But they look weird."

"Maybe they're supposed to be aliens from out of space."

"You mean in space."

"That's what I said."

"You said out of space."

"It's outer space. Not out of space."

"Whatever … look at him … over there. He looks like Napoleon."

"Who's that?"

"He's French."

"No, I mean. Who is that over there?"

"That's Parker and Portia! They're supposed to be in a rock 'n roll band."

"They look more like Donny and Marie Osmond."

"Who are they?"

"Pop singers from a long time ago."

"No, I mean. Who is that over there?"

"Who?"

"Way over there by the building …"

"You mean that bowling ball?"

"Is that what that is? How come he has holes in his body?"

"That's where you're supposed to put your fingers, to hold the ball. Haven't you seen bowling on television?"

"Where's Panic?" I asked, interrupting whoever was talking.

"I don't know. Who cares?"

"I know, right," exclaimed Pashelle. It was so annoying. She kept stealing my line.

Over the next thirty minutes or so, pumpkins slowly cleared the buildings in the Eye, and pretty soon, before I knew it, most of the pumpkins were outside in the Eye gardens. It was time. The opening ceremony was about to start. We could tell because they were testing the loudspeaker microphone, which created this eerie, witch-like sound.

Quite a few elders had gathered on a temporary, makeshift stage set up in the Green Garden. They were taking their seats. I wondered if they were all going to speak into the microphone. Once the microphone was operating properly, Elected Elder One stood up and approached the front of the stage. He would give a speech now. He was our leader. His name was Pudge Pumpkin. Everyone quieted down.

Actually his voice was not very loud or strong. He had throat problems starting a few years back. And he'd always had health problems ever since I'd known him. So he would only say a couple of things and would then introduce Ms. Pumpkin, who has been giving the public speeches and announcements for the past little while.

"Hello. Welcome." And there was a roar, so loud that I wondered whether the ghouls who were taking a nap heard us. He had to pause and wait for the noise to calm before speaking again. And just as well because he needed to take a big intake of breath. And in his loudest of voices, which was not very loud, he said, "I officially announce that Halloween is on!"

And that announcement was met by an even more raucous cheer. This time I was certain the ghouls had heard. Halloween had been "on" for quite some time now. But Halloween doesn't officially begin until the opening ceremony.

Ms. Pumpkin was now on stage. She is an Elected Elder. Her given name is Patricia.

"Well, don't we all look wonderful," she began. She was dressed up as a queen from the olden British times. Her tiara was almost as bright as the sun itself.

"Are those real diamonds?" I asked Pannette.

"Sssshhhhh," she said.

I don't like it when pumpkins ignore me. Couldn't she have at least acknowledged my question?

"For you pumpkins who are trick-or-treating for the very first time, to you pumpkins who are for the very last time, and to all pumpkins going out, tonight you will embark on a journey that will create a lifetime of memories and dreams. Your travels today will stay with you for as long as you live."

And so her speech started. Her voice echoed through the Eye Gardens.

We had a long time to wait. We were out second to last. Wow. Maybe next year I would ask someone if we could go first. I wonder if we can make requests like that. I felt a little jealous of the pumpkins all dressed up in their costumes, standing near the West Gate.

Ms. Pumpkins' speech was going on a long time. She was going on about the meaning of Halloween. Why we celebrate it. How important it is to us. Its origins and history. And even talking outside the topic of Halloween at times. She spent a great deal of time recognizing the great pumpkins of our past and acknowledging their achievements.

It was really interesting, although I think most of us wished it had ended by now. And on and on and on she went. I was kind of in and out, sometimes paying attention, other times not. I was looking around at all the pumpkins dressed up and ready to go trick-or-treating. I was starting to get restless. I started playing with my witch teeth. Four-year-old pumpkins don't have much patience. Pashelle was aiming her bracelets at various pumpkins, pretending missiles were being released. I was glad we were sitting down, at least, relaxed on a bench.

"So in conclusion ..." she continued.

Like isn't that the third time she had said "in conclusion"? Oh, you don't know. Sorry. Well, I don't really want to recite the whole speech word for word, do I? If you are really interested in it, as I am sure you are, then you can probably find a copy of it online somewhere, on your computer. Like they do on television.

Once the speech finally did end, she handed the stage to another Ms. Pumpkin, who reminded us of the instructions we should follow at this point. Ms. Pumpkin is the Elected Elder who was in charge of coordinating all the activities associated with Halloween this

year. Her given name is Poppy. She started out by going over the
basic rules of trick-or-treating and what was expected of us in the
city. Yes, like hello, it was on the test. We all passed the test. It's not
rocket science.

After her lecture finished, there was a small display of fireworks.
That was exciting. Big, bright lights shooting up in the air, some
making their way up into the sky and then back down, while others
quiet at first but then exploding into the sky. And there was a lot of
"ooohhhing" and "aaahhhing" when each one did something. Some
of the fireworks didn't do anything at all, though. I think those ones
are called duds. It's a show of might. A show that incites pride in
us, to remind us of who we are. It also serves as a test of the system
to ensure that it's working properly. The fireworks show went on
for about twenty minutes. We don't want anything to go wrong
at crunch time, do we? We all know Wanda and her followers are
hovering up in the sky, somewhere, watching us. The fireworks
concluded the opening ceremony, although no one actually said the
opening ceremony was finished.

"Come on, let's move back, over there." Pannette pointed near a
tree way out in the Lily Garden.

"You know what? We could probably get back into the lounge if
we can get out of here."

"Yeah, come on. Let's push our way through." This was a good
suggestion. I mean, if everyone was outside, then maybe no one was
in the lounge now.

And so we made our way to the main entrance through the
clusters of pumpkins all going in different directions. There were
still lots of pumpkins inside the activity center, that's for sure. I guess
some preferred to stay warm than to listen to those lectures.

I'll say one thing. Sure was a festive atmosphere around here.
Very difficult to describe the excitement on all our faces. It was a

different feeling compared with previous years. When I was one year old, I didn't even know what was going on. Even the last two years, it was as if I didn't really care or understand. I remember wondering what all the commotion was about. All I knew was that we had lots of candy in supply afterward. But this year I'm actually going out and getting it. And the whole thing is not about the candy anymore, as it was in past years, but more about the adventure.

"Oh, it's you!" I heard Pashelle yell, as we approached the lounge.

I quickly scanned the lounge to see how busy it was and then took a second glance to see if there were any available seats, but there were none. The lounge seats about forty pumpkins, with comfortable standing room for another seventy or so.

I wondered who Pashelle was pointing to. Not only was I not paying attention to her, we were all wearing costumes, so it was difficult to tell for certainty who anyone really was.

"Who's that?"

"It's Panic."

Is it really? Who? Which one? No one really responded or took notice of her, despite the fact that she screamed it out. It was really noisy in there, the words echoing through the room. This was one of the newer buildings in the Patch and one of the few made of wood. Actually very light wood, creating this echo. The ceiling was quite high and pointed. Kind of like my hat.

"Really? Who?"

"The Werewolf. There." She pointed near the fireplace.

I thought to myself, How does she know? And even if it is Panic, what is she going to do? Even she wouldn't start a brawl just as the opening ceremony had ended.

"Just leave it alone," Pannette said, raising her eyeballs, hoping the topic of conversation was going to be different.

We walked into the brightly lit room and walked over to the

other side of the fireplace, and I leaned against a wall. There were no seats available.

We spent the next little while looking out the window, toward the West Gate, watching as pumpkins left the grounds of the Eye. Slowly the lounge cleared enough that we were all able to sit down. By this time, Polo and Plato had come into the lounge and joined us. Polo said they had been assigned to clean up duty for two weeks, as punishment for causing a "public scene." That means, for two hours each day they had to go around and pick up garbage and any mess made in the Eye. Plato wasn't happy with Polo at all. It looked like those two had been arguing and fighting. I actually don't blame Plato in the least. I doubt very much that he wanted to cause a public scene.

Peter appeared soon after. He walked to where we were and sat down. He didn't even bother saying hello to anyone. Shouldn't he say hello? That's Peter for you. I mean, I'm always social. Always saying hello and greeting everyone. Asking pumpkins how they were and stuff. His ghost costume was covering his face, so you couldn't even see him properly. I wondered what the odds were of us all sitting here together at this moment, after the trouble we were getting into. Peter seemed to have given up on his disappointment about being "forced" to come with us. Pannette asked him what the Elected Elders had said. Peter said he had received no punishment at all. Amazing. He was told that even though it had been dangerous for him to leave the group like that, he was given only a warning. Well, someone in the office must really like him. Or feel sorry for him.

We continued to wait, idly chatting about nothing interesting in particular. It was kind of like the calm before the storm. Pannette spent a considerable time explaining what she would have to do in the coming weeks volunteering in the hospital. Maybe she would learn something about medicine. Maybe she would become so interested in medicine that she would become a doctor. I wondered what

I would be when I grew up. I wouldn't want to be a guard. That job would be too hard for little me. What if I had to break up a fight? I might accidentally get punched in the nose. That couldn't be an option. Well, no sense in stressing myself about that now.

I watched Pashelle and Polo practice their superhero powers on each other. I wonder who would win in a real fight, Superman or Wonder Woman? Polo never seems to take an interest in me. He likes talking to Pashelle. It kind of makes me feel jealous. Sometimes I would ask him questions, and if Pashelle was standing next to me, he would answer the question to her. Yet it was me who had asked it. Whenever Pashelle left my side, he would leave too. I could never say or do anything that interested him. I think he thinks I'm boring. I think he likes her aggressive behavior. And he was so aggressive that day. He never said he touched Panic, but Plato confirmed that Polo pushed Panic against the tree.

It seemed like hours had passed, but I know it wasn't hours.

And then the fireworks went off again, out of the blue. It was a sudden, loud noise that surprised us. That could only mean one thing. The first pumpkins had come back from trick-or-treating. Wow. Can you believe that? Pashelle went back to the window that provides a view of the West Gate. She thought it was Priscilla Pumpkin and her group, as they were the first to leave the Eye, and would be the first to reenter. Their containers full of candy, I bet.

We all got up and were able to find seats near the window. And after watching the next handful of groups come back, I suggested we go outside. The West Gate was the place to be.

"Let's go out. Our time must be coming up."

"It probably is. How much longer do we have to wait? Look at all the pumpkins who have come back home." I had taken out my false teeth earlier but was thinking I should put them back in again. It was difficult having a conversation with them in my mouth. Just as we left the lounge, we were approached by Ms. Pumpkin, who instructed us to get ready. We walked toward Halloween Headquarters to sign out. We waited in line behind Pod and Pol.

"Hey, we should be in front of you guys," I joked to them. Not that it really mattered at that point. The real order line was outside. How many pumpkins in front of us? I started to count. It looked like there were six groups ahead of us.

The line moved slowly. I wondered if Portia was up front, again. There were only two groups behind us. I didn't recognize who they were. You might think it strange that I didn't know everyone in the Patch, but don't forget, I'm only four years old. I don't even know all the four-year-olds.

When we got to the table, it was our turn to register. This was our first check-out point. We told Ms. Pumpkin our names, and we had to put a check mark beside our names on the listing. Next, we had our picture taken. Mr. Pumpkin took our picture. We made sure we looked our very best. Pannette had to help me with my face stitches. And I helped to ensure that her bandages were inside her dress. Mr. Pumpkin made us laugh. Pashelle, Pannette, Pavneet, and I knelt down on the ground, while Peter, Polo, and Plato stood behind us. He actually took three pictures. I tried to look scary in the first two but ended up with a big smile on my face by the time he took the third. That was fun. We were told the copies would be available the next day.

We collected our orange containers, shaped like pumpkins, of course, and we went out the main entrance and headed west until we reached the Green Garden. We stopped at the barrier and were met by security guards. Here, we had to form into a real and proper line. So we waited for two groups to line up ahead of us. Then we stood behind Party, Payne, and Perry. Then Pod and Pol took up their places behind us.

"We passed you," I said to Pod. The line moved along slowly, inching ahead, until we reached the makeshift stage. When it was our turn, we went onto the stage. This was the second check-out point. Again, we had to tell the guards our names. And the guards put check marks on their lists.

Then we walked down from the stage, moving ahead in a singular line, through the paths of the Green Garden, then through the paths of the Rose Garden, until we reached the West Gate. This was the third check-out point. Here, we were greeted by Pudge and other Elected Elders, who took the roll call once again. Pudge wished us good luck and told us to have fun. We watched Party, Payne, and Perry leave the Eye and head out going south on column CD03.

Wow. We were next. It was only a few more minutes now.

CHAPTER 9
TRICK-OR-TREAT

We walked down column CD03, unaccompanied by any guards at this point, as we were told there would be numerous guards on the trick-or-treat route itself. We knew the route. It was on the test. As we walked south, we could see the faces of the pumpkins who had finished walking past us. Some of them looked tired. I didn't think I would be tired when I came back. I wished I could trick-or-treat all night. I could see that their containers were overflowing with candy.

None of us had entered the city from the South Exit before. I had wandered down this far south on this column only once and had stopped well short of actually viewing the exit up close. It was a long walk. And we were moving quickly, just so that we could see Party and his friends up ahead. We reached the South Exit trees, which are some of the tallest trees in the land. I looked up and almost got dizzy staring up at the highest branches at the top. We walked through a narrow path that wound in between these trees.

Unlike the East Gate, this exit is actually a bridge. It's a ten-minute stroll over a very secure brick bridge, which was built hundreds of years ago. The bridge itself is not very high off the ground, and the water underneath is very shallow. This is where Star River leaves the Patch. Once we got off the bridge, we were met by more guards. And it had now been close to an hour since we started our trek from the Eye. This was our fourth and final check-out point. We were not required to resubmit our names, however. We left the trees behind us and walked across a very small park, and up ahead we could see people's houses. We were now finally in the residential area of New Surrey City.

There were hundreds of ghouls floating in the sky. They were laughing and trying to scare us at the same time. I had never seen this many ghouls all gathered at the same place at the same time. It was like a ghoul party. We knew there would be lots of them in the sky, but to be honest, we had no idea there would be this many.

And all we saw were houses. Big and tall houses. This was where people lived. And we nervously looked at each other. As if to say, "What do we do now?" Suddenly, and without consulting with us, Pashelle burst out from our group and ran to the first house she saw. She ran up the driveway. Once she reached the front door, she jumped up as high as she could and smashed her hand against the doorbell. We ran after her.

We were standing outside the front door where these people lived, and we were waiting for them to open the door.

"What are we going say when they open the door?" asked Polo. The question kind of took me by surprise. We knew what we were going to say. We had been trained for this moment since birth. It was a stupid question but a logical question at the same time. In all my life, I don't think I have ever been as nervous as I was at that moment. We all were.

Then the door opened. We looked up to see the person's face, and we said the only thing we knew to say. We said the only thing we were taught to say. We yelled as loud as our lungs would allow,

"Trick or treat!" And since Peter had just come up the driveway, he said "Trick or treat!" all by himself.

We held out our containers, and the man said how nice and scary our costumes were and slowly put candy in our containers. We all said, "Thank you" and then he quietly closed the door.

That was fun. That was a riot. I couldn't believe how easy that was. It was as natural to us as breathing the air.

"What did you get?"

"Mars bar."

"What about you?"

"I got a Mars bar, too."

"Same with me."

"We all got the same thing?"

"Who cares … come on."

So we ran down that driveway onto the main road, which was named Strathorn Avenue, up the driveway of the next-nearest house. Four of us jumped up and hit the doorbell this time. The door opened, and again we yelled "Trick or treat!"

And again Peter was late. This time, no excuse.

"Come on, Peter. Say it with the rest of us. Walk faster."

And this was the way it went. Pashelle, Polo, and Plato were usually first to the house, and they rang the bell. Pannette, Pavneet, and I ran up soon after, just in time to yell, "Trick or treat," with Peter following up behind us. Sometimes he arrived in time to say "Trick or treat" with us in unison, but most times he didn't. A few times he was so late in arriving at the door of the house, that he didn't even say those words at all.

All the people were so nice. For the most part, they seemed just as happy to give us candy as we were to receive it. Some people even gave us two pieces at a time!

Some houses we skipped over. We were told that if the house lights were not turned on, that meant there was no one home, and we didn't even need to ring the doorbell. At some houses, the doorbell was too high to reach, so instead we banged on the door.

We had finished all the houses on Strathorn Avenue, turned left, and walked along Windsor Street. At this point, we must have knocked on at least ten houses, if not more.

"No. Don't do that," I suddenly heard from behind me.

It was Peter. Someone had just taken his candy container. He had just been robbed! Right in front of our eyes. Actually, Peter was behind us, and none of us saw what happened. But oh my goodness. What a traumatic event that must have been for him. It was a witch. Peter said that the witch came out of nowhere on her broom, swooped in, and grabbed the container. Oh, some ghouls can be so cruel. Such meanies. So now all of Peter's candy was gone. He looked so shocked. He looked like he was ready to cry.

"Oh, don't worry. Luckily we just started, so you didn't have much. Go to the guard." I looked around to see where the guard was stationed. The elders had told us that extra guards were being kept back at the Patch this year, and thus there would be fewer in the city. And since many pumpkins were actually finished, there were even fewer guards on the city streets. I glanced up and down the street to find one.

"Look! There, Peter. Across the street. There." I pointed at the guard in the distance. "Go get another container. Quick. And then just stay there. Don't come back this way to try to catch up. Just cross this street, and by the time we finish these houses and come up that street, we will meet you. Do you understand?"

He nodded. How could he be so careless like that?

"Hold on to your bag tighter. And try to keep up with us." I think we were all moving too fast for him. I started to think it might have been better if he had gone with the communal group, after all. Was I going to have to watch him the whole time?

"Hey. Hey, you guys. We need to slow down," I yelled to my friends up ahead.

Pashelle, Pavneet, and Pannette stopped. Polo and Plato, however, did not. They were too far ahead of us for them even to bother to wait. It looked like they had caught up to Party, Payne, and Perry.

"We need to stay together. Pashelle, you're going too fast," I told her.

"I'm just trying to keep up with everyone else," she explained.

"No, Pashelle. Just keep up with us," I said.

"You should keep up with us. Look, now we're last." She didn't want to slow down. In reality, neither did Pannette or I.

While we had stopped on the street discussing our pace, Pod and Pol had passed us. "Still behind us, Petrina." Pod was half-joking, and half-bragging.

"No worries. If we're out here longer than you, that just means we're going to get more candy." Actually that was not true. The only way we would get more candy was if we started repeating houses. We might be the last pumpkins, but there were plenty of other trick-or-treaters on the street. It was now covered with children. It was dark enough for them to start. I think they have later bedtimes than we do. Besides, they are not afraid of the ghouls like we are.

"Well, Pavneet is not feeling that well, is she? So you keep up with us," Pannette said in a calmer voice. She had noticed that Pavneet was starting to tire. At least Pashelle didn't run after Polo and Plato.

"Okay. But we can't just stand here wasting time," she reluctantly agreed. "Who took Peter's candy? Was it a witch?"

"I don't know. That's what he said."

So we marched onward, all agreeing to stay together. Which should have been the plan from the start. Besides, the initial excitement had worn off. There was no need to go that fast. We managed to finish the houses on this side of the street, crossed, and met Peter up ahead.

So on to the next house. "Trick or treat."

Coming down the driveway from that house, Peter bumped right into me from behind, and my container flipped over, and some of the candy came out and fell onto the ground. What a goof.

"Watch where you're going."

"Don't touch that one," he warned.

"Why?"

"It fell on the ground."

"So? These ones are wrapped in paper."

"It doesn't matter. You know the rules. Those need to be set aside."

"Peter's right, Petrina. Just leave these ones."

What, like since when did Pannette start taking sides with my brother? How lame.

"These ones have wrappers. None of them touched the ground. Okay?"

I ignored them, put the two lollipops and the one Aero chocolate back in my container, and for a change I was the first one to jump up and ring the next doorbell.

We continued onward, completing the row of houses on the whole street. We found ourselves walking quite slowly and making sure we stayed together. Pavneet was tiring even more. Peter always seemed tired. We were walking too slowly. And the more we slowed, the more it seemed we were getting farther behind the pumpkins up ahead.

So Pashelle returned to the speed we had when we first started. Pannette and I kept up with her. Peter and Pavneet were one house behind, and pretty soon they were two houses behind. I heard Peter yell, "Slow down!" and "Wait for us!" But I didn't want to wait any-more. Pannette, Pashelle and I were having too much fun. We were racing onward. But it didn't seem like we were catching up to Groups 40 and 42 up ahead.

Next door … "Trick or treat!"
Next door … "Trick or treat!"
Next door … "Trick or treat!"

As we turned the corner to the next row of houses, the pumpkins up ahead had turned another corner themselves, and they were out of sight. We were the last ones out. All we could see now were children, and they were racing past us the way the hare raced past the tortoise.

We had a map showing which way we were supposed to walk, but who looks at a map? Everyone says you just follow the leader. If we have lost contact with those ahead, however, that is reason to refer to our map. The guards were nowhere in sight, either. I didn't think we were lost, but I did think we should look at our map.

"Hey, guys, who has the map?"

"Peter."

I turned to see if I could locate Peter and Pavneet. But they were nowhere close.

"Why does he have the map?"

"I don't know. Someone has to hold on to it. Did you ask the guard for it?"

"When?"

"When we checked out at headquarters."

No, I hadn't. I had thought Pannette would have gotten it. Or even Plato. How did we let Peter have our map? Who gave him that responsibility?

"Yeah … but … let's wait for them."

"I can't even see them. They're so far behind."

"Why do we need to look at the map?" asked Pashelle. She was in denial that we were lost.

"Do you know where we are? Which way we are supposed to go?"

As we looked around, we also noticed that the fog was starting to get thicker. There was still no rain, but it was getting colder.

After we waited for a few minutes, we did finally see them. They were walking very slowly. They were about five houses behind us. We stopped and let them catch up to us. Even Pashelle thought this was the right thing to do, at this point.

"Let's see the map, Peter," I ordered him, as they finally caught up with us.

"You guys are going so fast," said Pavneet. "Do you think it's time to go back home?"

"Where's the map?" I had to ask Peter again.

"I hope I didn't lose it," he said with considerable doubt that he even had it. He was searching through all his clothes and his sac.

"What? How could you lose the map? And why do you have our map in the first place? Who gave it to you?"

"No, I have it. It's here somewhere. I put it right in here."

"Peter, we need that map now. Why do you even have it? Answer me."

"I was the only one in our group who was near the guard when he was handing them out. He gave me a map and gave me the flashlight."

He was now checking the same places in his clothes that he had already checked. Great, now no map.

"Found it."

"What a relief."

"I know, right."

We all let out a collective sigh. We quickly studied the map and found our place from the street names, and we were able to figure out which way we should go. There was an orange line with an arrow on the map, indicating the route. And we were all in agreement where we were and which way we should walk. So onward we went.

Next door ... "Trick or treat!"

Next door ... "Trick or treat!"

Next door ... "Trick or treat!"

This was great. I was having a really great time. I have to admit, though, that it was getting kind of scary out there, all alone in the city, with no other pumpkins in sight. And this was our first time trick-or-treating. And we constantly had to slow down for Pavneet and Peter. We were getting a little annoyed with them. Pavneet did not look well. And it was getting foggier still. This was scary but exciting at the same time. Pannette suggested that we skip the rest of the houses and just go back to the Patch right away. She made it sound as if she were serious, but in fact she was really kidding. She was having a blast.

It was Pashelle who said, "No way."

Pavneet asked if we had far to go. I offered that we didn't have very far to go. It was only up this street, then right and back over the bridge. At least that was what I hoped. We agreed to continue.

CHAPTER 10
HOUSE

Onward we went to the next house. "Trick or treat!" we all said. "Wow," said the old lady. "You all scared me." And she continued. "But you know what, dears? I have run out of candy to give you. It's just such a shame. And I don't have any other treats I can give you. I knew I should have kept more, but the knocks on the door kept coming, and I don't know what to say."

"That's okay," we said collectively, and we turned and were about to go to the next house.

"Oh, but wait. I have an idea," she started again. "I have some freshly baked delicious chocolate chip cookies in the oven right now. And I think they're almost done. Would you like some of those cookies? Why don't you come inside and wait?"

"Okay," Pashelle agreed, without any consultation.

"No," Peter said.

I love chocolate chip cookies. They are my favorite treat. The pumpkin chefs are always baking peanut butter or oatmeal or some other different type of cookie. These ones would be hot and right out of the oven, too.

"All of you. It's only going to take a few more minutes. Come inside. It's warmer."

"Let's go inside and just warm up and rest a minute, Petrina. I'm getting tired. I kind of want to go home now too," Pavneet said again.

I could tell she wanted to sit down and rest and get warmed up.

"We should just keep going," Peter said again.

"Okay. We'll wait for the cookies," Pashelle blurted out, and, without any further hesitation, she walked right into the woman's house.

Aw, I thought to myself. The rest of us were taken aback. Shocked, almost, that Pashelle was standing inside the house, near the stairs to the second level. Either we go inside and get Pashelle, or go inside and wait with Pashelle. Heck, we could even leave her there. Well, we couldn't do that. Pannette took a couple of steps toward the door and looked like she was going inside. So I did the same thing as Pashelle. I walked right into the house. This was the first time I had been inside a person's house. And it looked magical. There were lots of lights, and candles everywhere. Very spacious, and plenty of places to sit down. The floor was soft underneath my feet, which were sore after walking on the hard pavement. That, in itself, was worth coming inside. Pannette followed me in.

"Come here. Sit down," the woman suggested. She seemed very sweet. Looking up at her face, I could see she was really old because her skin was wrinkly and soft.

She led us to a room where we could sit. I looked outside through the door and saw Pavneet push away Peter's hand and slowly and cautiously walk inside, leaving only Peter outside. He was trying to get my attention, nodding his head out to the right, as if to say, "Let's go." Let's get out of here, he was thinking. I ignored him, and we sat squished together on the same chair. We really don't take up much room.

"There, you all look so wonderful. I should take a picture of you.

Come on, you scary ghost," the woman said, walking toward Peter and grabbing the door handle, basically hinting to him that if he didn't come inside, she was locking him out. Peter had little choice but to come in. He stood against the wall.

"And what is your name?" she asked of no one in particular.

"My name is Pashelle Pumpkin."

"Oh, what a lovely name."

"It's so warm in here," whispered Pavneet, snuggling up next to my body, grasping one of my arms. She looked so relaxed and peaceful. A big grin on her face.

"Let me go into the kitchen and check on those cookies. They must be done by now. You wait right here." And the woman went back into the kitchen.

"We should get out of here. Really. This is not a good idea. We could get into trouble," Peter pleaded with us.

"Just for a minute," I could hear Pavneet say in a very soft voice. The rest of us ignored his request. I mean, who cares what he says?

"We're not going to get into trouble. And you're not going to tell anyone, are you?" Pashelle asked Peter threateningly.

"It's so bright in here. This is so cool." Pannette, like me, was amazed at all the light and beauty of the decorations.

"I know, right." Pashelle was also in agreement.

"Don't fall asleep, Pavneet. We're just going to eat and then we're going."

We all nodded.

And just then, the scariest thing happened. The woman came out of the kitchen, all clad in orange sheets, holding two large knives, one in each hand.

And she yelled, "I'm gonna have me some fresh pumpkin pie!"

And it was like, what does that mean? What is she going to do to us?

"She wants to carve us up! Run!"

Pavneet woke up in a hurry and found energy that I had not seen from her in days. She vaulted off the chair, ran for the door, and leaped up to the handle to see if she could turn it. Just then, Peter grabbed one of the many lit candles in the room and flung it at the woman. And would you believe that he missed, standing not even three feet away from her? How feeble, I thought.

But at least it gave us the idea. We had to act fast. We each picked up candles and started throwing them at her, one by one. We threw at least ten lit candles at her. She managed to elude them all, except one, and her orange outfit finally caught on fire at the hem. That gave us enough time to escape, and we raced to the back of the house, looking for a door, or any opening to get back outside. We jumped on tables, chairs, and counters, trying to open any window, but without any luck. We were trapped. We had nowhere to go. Trapped in a house with a deranged old woman who had a craving for pumpkin pie.

"What do we do now? She wants to eat us."

And for the second consecutive day, Pavneet threw out her seeds. Poor Pavneet. Poor us.

"Let's hide in this closet. It's not opening."

"She's coming!"

As the woman was approaching from one end of the house, Pashelle ran around the other side of the wall, back to the front of the house, and started climbing up the stairs. We all followed. We managed to make it up the stairs and went into a room, and all together we managed to close the door. Not sure how much good that would do, though, because we didn't know how to lock it. It was only a matter of time before the woman would come upstairs and grab a hold of us.

"Okay. So now what?"

"Let's just hide."

Before we took cover, we searched the room for anything we could use to defend ourselves with. And we couldn't really find anything to use. Too bad there were no lit candles here. We were in big, big trouble. No doubt about that.

"I have an idea. I think if one of us gives up and surrenders, she might let the rest of us go. Someone would have to provide an offering to her," Peter suggested.

We all looked at each other, and we gave it a thought. Not the worst idea. We had to do something.

"I will. I'm so tired now, anyway. I'm only going to slow you down in any escape." Pavneet thought that was the best solution.

"No!" shouted Pannette. "There has to be a better way."

"I know where you're hiding, my sweet little pumpkins. I'm coming to find you." She was now up the stairs, and it was just a matter of time before she opened the door.

"Look. I found a candle," said Pannette. She had found one in an open box.

"Okay. So now we need to put fire on it. We need a fire lighter."

"Look, these things are matches. Didn't Mr. Pumpkin say that matches can make fire?"

"Okay. Let's try. Let's make the fire."

"Okay. Let's do it. How?"

Pannette started to read the instructions from the box. Seemed fairly simple. "Strike the match against the side of the box." So Pashelle and I took out a match from the box and slid it slowly and carefully across the rough edge of the box. We waited for a second, but nothing happened.

"It didn't work."

"Try it again. Quick. She's coming this way now."

"You must be in here." She had found us.

We swiped the match again, and still no fire. Strange because this time we rubbed the match even more carefully.

"We must be doing it wrong."

"Maybe these are dud matches, like dud fireworks."

"We need to do this more quickly."

"We know we need to do this quickly."

And in haste and being in sheer panic mode, we rubbed the match against the side of the box much faster this time. And just as soon as we swung that match over the rough edge of the box, the match created fire. This scared Pashelle out of her wits, so much so that she let go of it and fell backward. I was so scared of the fire that I just let go of the match out of sheer fright. Peter and Pannette replaced Pashelle and me, and now they were holding the lit match. The fire took us so much by surprise that we forgot what to do with it. Peter and Pannette twirled around, making two or three full circles with the match, clutching it with trepidation, and hoping they, themselves, wouldn't catch on fire. And while they were still in full motion, they accidentally let go of the match just as the woman opened the door. The match was flung with so much force that it reached the height of her face, and it distracted her. Pashelle got up and leaped at her feet to bite her ankle, and the woman lost her balance. As she tried leaning sideways to regain her balance, she hit her head against a strong, sharp, pointed board next to the door and abruptly slid down the side of the wall.

Extraordinary!

The scene was chaotic. The match was in her hair, although the fire had burned out. It was a miraculous circumstance. We couldn't believe what had just happened. We stared at each other, wondering what we should do.

The woman lay on the ground, face down. She wasn't moving. Her eyes were closed.

"Is she dead?" Pashelle asked, lying next to her, avoiding the crush of the weight of her body.

"Who cares? Let's get out of here."

"Let's burn her first," Pashelle said, grabbing another match out of the box.

"No, we're not, Pashelle. Put those matches down."

We left the room, slid down the stairs, and took hold of our candy containers.

"How are we going to get out?"

"Let's try throwing this lamp at the window. Maybe the window will break."

"Good idea," I said.

So we all managed to lift up a very heavy lamp. And on a count of three, we were going to fling it at the window. But apparently Peter can't count, and he let go at the count of two. This caused us to lose momentum, and the lamp fell on the floor and broke in half.

We were frustrated. I was frustrated with Peter.

"Well, at least we don't have a heavy lamp to lift this time. And this much might be enough if we're able to throw it fast and hard enough."

We were able to lift this half piece of very hard wood much more easily than the full lamp. And we threw it, almost like an arrow, at the window right next to the front door. The sound of it hitting the window was loud enough, and it cracked the window glass, but it didn't create a big enough hole for us to escape. Plus, we didn't hit the window in the middle. So we picked up what amounted to a wooden spear a second time and flung it again. And then a third and a fourth time. And on the fourth time, the glass shattered enough that a hole was created just big enough that we were able to use the spear to break apart the glass. It was now big enough that we could get through.

"Okay. Good. Now who's first?"

Why even ask ourselves? We knew Pashelle was going first. She slowly twisted her body through the hole and fell down on the ground outside. I was next. I was able to get through without getting a cut anywhere on my body. But Pavneet was not so lucky. As she jumped through the window, she misjudged the distance and ending up getting a small scrape on her skin from the glass before falling down onto the front lawn.

"This day only seems to getting better for you, Pavneet."

"Trick-or-treating is like fighting a war."

It was good to see that at least she was keeping her sense of humor.

Before Peter came out, we made him pass the candy containers to us on the other side. For the most part, we were able to catch the containers with most of the candy still trapped inside. We picked up the rest and put them in the containers. Yet another trick-or-treat violation.

Wow. What an unbelievable experience that was. We could have been killed. We could have been turned into pumpkin pies!

"No one ever says anything about what just happened. To anyone. Ever."

We all agreed.

CHAPTER 11
LOST

The first thing we noticed when we got back onto the street was how foggy it was. It was dark too. The sun was completely out of view. The fog was inescapable. We could hardly see each other. It was too late for us to be out. We were in the city all alone. All the other pumpkins were long gone. The shrieks of the witches were getting louder, and nearer. The ghouls were flying so low, we could feel the wind as they went by. Back in the Patch, when you hear those shrieks at night, it's more like an echo through the tall trees. But out here, they are real, and close by. They sounded like a roar. And it was Halloween night.

It didn't seem like there was anyone here, except us and the ghouls. Even if there were others outside, it was so foggy that we couldn't see.

"Where's the flashlight? Turn it on."

Peter searched his sac for the flashlight. He couldn't find it. It must have fallen out in the house. Well, that's just great. We wondered whether we should go back into the house and get it. What if the woman woke up?

Then, all of a sudden, from out in the distance came beautiful sounds. They were whistles. Pumpkin whistles. They were coming. They had found us. Oh, what a relief! I didn't say this before, but let me say it now: I think we were lost. I couldn't tell you if we should have gone straight or right or left, or even back the way we came. We wouldn't even have been able to read the map because of all the fog, and there was no light.

"That's it. Trick-or-treating is finished," Pashelle said, letting out a sigh of relief, but also with a bit of disappointment. I think she wanted to be out there all night, collecting more candy, whether or not there had been a disaster at the woman's house.

"We're over here," we yelled.

Anywhere from twelve to fifteen elders came into view, from up the street. Apparently, a search-and-rescue committee had been organized to find us. We had sent the Patch into a state of worry. And you know what? They should have been worried. We were in big trouble out here by ourselves.

"Okay. Settle down, everyone. Is everyone here? I see Pannette. Petrina, yes? Good."

"I'm here. It's Pashelle."

"Yes, I know it's you. Good." Mr. Pumpkin probably thought this was all her fault. And it probably was. If she hadn't gone into the house, I don't think any of this would have happened.

"Where are Peter and Pavneet? Polo and Plato are accounted for. Peter ..."

The only ones who responded were ghouls.

"Peter!"

"Pavneet!"

"Pavneet, where are you?"

"They were here just seconds ago. Peter, where did you go?" I wondered out aloud.

This was crazy. Where did they go? They were right there. Peter had been directly in front of me, looking for the flashlight. I couldn't have turned my head for more than a second.

We all screamed out their names. But there was no answer. Well, this was weird. This was starting to scare me. Like, big-time. We spread out to call their names, but still no response. After a few minutes, Mr. Pumpkin told us to go back to the Patch. Like, no way was I going back there without Peter and Pavneet.

"I want to help look for them."

"No, Petrina," I was told. "You have no experience in search-and-rescue missions. You could put yourself, and us, in danger. You must go back to the Patch. We'll find them both, and we will bring them home."

I yelled, "Peter!" about as loud as I have ever yelled anything in my life. The return silence was so deafening, it nearly burst my eardrums. Oh, where are you, Peter?

With all the shrieks of the ghouls echoing through the buildings and houses, it was not likely they would have heard us anyway, even if they did only wander off mistakenly just a little ways down the street.

"Like, I'm not joking, Mr. Pumpkin. They were standing right here just a minute ago." I started to get so scared that I began to tremble and shake. I began to cry.

Pannette put her arm around me and assured me that everything was going to be okay.

"Pannette, they were right here one minute ago. They couldn't have gone far."

"Come with me, you three," said Mr. Pumpkin, pushing us from behind. Elders were all around us. I couldn't escape them. It was like they were taking us prisoners or something. They should be helping look for Peter and Pavneet. How were they going to find them if they are standing around and escorting us back to the Patch? There was very little I could say or do, however, that would convince anyone I should stay and help in the search. I had to follow orders and not get emotional.

"Oh, please find them," was the last thing I remember saying, as we walked back up the street, in absolute disbelief about what had just happened. I couldn't stop wondering to myself if I would ever see them again. I felt completely numb inside. Of course the elders will find them, I thought to myself. They will come back home. I was confident. I was in disbelief. Was I in denial?

My body trembled as we walked through the trees of the South Exit, back over the bridge, and up along column CD03. By the time I walked into the main entrance and sat down, I was an emotional wreck. I was frozen and couldn't say a single word. I was as scared as I have ever been in my life.

Although everyone was glad to see me, there was naturally concern over Peter and Pavneet. Everyone was working quietly, still performing their duties. There were some who laughed quietly and seemed like they didn't even care about them at all, though. Like really, doesn't anyone care? I guess it's only a pumpkin, when it doesn't affect you directly. But it still made me feel more alone.

I sat motionless on that warm seat for what seemed like hours, staring out the window near the main entrance for any news.

The fireworks were still going off, making noise and causing lightning flashes in the sky. There was still a Halloween party going on. Pumpkins were stuffing themselves full of appetizers.

"You should go to the hospital and have a nurse take a look at you, Petrina," I barely heard Ms. Pumpkin say to me.

"Okay, I will." I imagined that was where Pannette and Pashelle had gone, since I didn't know where they were.

I couldn't move. I didn't want to move. I was so tired. I was so scared. I was so sad.

I closed my eyes.

CHAPTER 12
AND FOUND

"Did you like it?" I heard someone say to me. What? I thought. "Petrina, did you have fun?"

I opened my eyes and saw Pimi Pumpkin standing over me, asking me another question. "Tell me all about it, Petrina. I can't wait to go next year."

She wants to hear about my trick-or-treating experience. I can barely open my eyes, Pimi. I didn't know what to tell her. I'm sure she knew about everything that had happened.

"Not now, okay. I'll tell you later."

It wasn't as noisy now as it was before. I might have fallen asleep. As a matter of fact, there was only one pumpkin talking. Was it Peter? I couldn't see who was talking, because I was sitting, and I couldn't see through all the pumpkins who were gathered.

It was Peter! Was he okay? He was standing in the center of the main entrance, near the tables at Halloween Headquarters, with pumpkins all around him. How long had I slept? What time was it? Was I dreaming? Where did he come from? It seemed like he was okay. What a relief, I thought.

"Where's Pavneet?" I turned to ask Pimi. She had already left my side, however, and was in the crowd mingling, trying to hear Peter speak. It looked as though Peter had only been inside for a few minutes. Everyone was quiet and was listening to what he was saying. I had to stand and refocus my eyes to see him. This was the first time today that I had seen his face, without his costume.

"… then the witch just grabbed Pavneet. She was standing right next to me. I couldn't stop them. One of them pushed me down to the ground."

I listened very carefully and intently. It was almost the first time I had listened to him this carefully, actually really caring what he had to say.

"I didn't know what to do … I just got up and ran after them. They were moving so fast, though, and pretty soon I lost track of where they had gone. It was so dark, and there was so much fog. And just then, the Five witches came to me, and one of them said, 'Get on the broom, Peter. We know where they're taking your friend.' They came from out of nowhere. Everything was happening so fast. So I climbed onto the broom, and we starting flying in the air, over the city streets, until we reached a forested area. And looking down, all I could see was fog. Wera Witch said that Pavneet was probably down below—there, where we were. And so we started to fly closer to the ground, until the Five witches saw an orange glow. They could see clearly through the fog. We decided it must be Pavneet. We flew right down near the ground until we got really close. Pavneet was trapped and couldn't escape. So the Five witches tried to scare the other witches away. But that didn't completely work. Then the Five witches threw potions at them. And then they got scared. The witches scattered and left Pavneet by herself. I got off the broomstick, untied her from a tree, and then helped her onto the broom, and we escaped. They flew us all the way to the South Exit. And that's when I yelled out to Mr. Pumpkin. And then …"

Wow. What a story. A real-life story of courage. That was Peter? He did that?

Then I saw a face through the window of the main entrance. It was Pavneet. I waved to her to come inside, but instead she was waving to me, beckoning to me to come outside. By this time, my tears of sorrow had turned into tears of joy.

As soon as I got outside, I grabbed Pavneet and gave her a hug. And I hugged her so strongly and for so long. I didn't feel like letting go of her. I may never hold anyone that tightly for the rest of my entire life.

"It's okay, Petrina."

"Are you still sick? You still look so pale. Come inside."

"I can't. I've been instructed to stay at the hospital and rest. Can you believe it? There's a party going on here, and I've been sent to the hospital. They finally believe I'm sick. After all that. I got sick, apparently, from spending time with the ghosts and witches."

"What do you mean? You've been sick for days now."

"I wasn't sick, Petrina. Well, not really."

"What do you mean?"

"I can tell you."

We walked toward the Rose Garden and sat on a bench. There was no more fog. It was raining. A steady stream of falling wet water from the sky. So much so, it seemed to have washed away all the fog. I have always hated the rain, but for some reason, I didn't mind the rain this evening. At least I could see. The rain was beautiful and refreshing, and I let it soak into my skin.

"A few days ago, when Peter was visiting, he noticed this terrible smell. I didn't know what it was. Peter said it was odd-smelling. It was a terrible aroma. But maybe I was just used to it. I thought it might have been my roommates' bad-smelling laundry or something."

"What was it?"

"Well, we didn't know. I mean, I was throwing up the previous night and all that morning. So Peter took a sample of some food that was in the house. And he took it to the hospital. And tests were done on it. And we found out it was rat-killer spray."

"What?"

"You know. Spray we use to kill rats. That I had probably inhaled too much of it. And I was feeling dizzy and sick because of it. So I went to the hospital and got tests done on me."

"Why was there rat-killer poison in your house?"

"I don't know. But we told the Elected Elders, and they thought at first that I must have inhaled it somewhere else, not at home. Because, as you know, no one is allowed to have possession of this substance without approval. We told the Elected Elders it was the smell from my house. That someone inside was using it, but they refused to believe us. They said they might do a surprise inspection, but there was no guarantee. That it could be days before it could be proven."

"Pansy had rat-killer poison. Remember …"

"That's right, Petrina. He did. He used it when we went out the East Gate. Peter threw the rat at Pansy, to prove he had that spray. And Mr. Pumpkin was there as a witness."

"Peter threw the rat?"

"Yes. And we proved it."

"Aw! They tried to poison you? Why didn't you tell me before?"

"I don't know. I didn't know what to say. I didn't want anyone to be scared. So Dr. Pumpkin prescribed some medicine. There's nothing wrong with me. They said all I needed was rest, and to make sure that I took the medicine."

"You were sick. And I kept telling you to hurry up …"

"I would have done the same thing as you."

For some reason, I didn't believe her. I don't think she would have left me behind, like we left her behind. I felt ashamed.

"Peter saved me, Petrina. I thought I was going to die. I thought the witches were going to eat me. And they probably would have, if it wasn't for my hero. Peter is my big brother. And you are my sister. You two are the only real family I have."

She explained how she heard the pumpkin whistles and how happy she was that we were going home. Between the antibiotics and sleeping pills, the only reason she had even made it that far, was from sheer adrenaline. This was the most important night of her life, and she didn't want to miss it. She didn't want to slow us down. As soon as she heard the whistles, however, she was picked up by a witch. And she was flown across the city to a nearby park. She couldn't have been there for long. They were trying to tie her to a tree so she couldn't move. Then Peter jumped down from the sky, grabbed her, and put her on the broom. And then they flew back. Wow. And I thought I had an experience that day. Not even close to what Pavneet had gone through.

"And Peter really saved you. You must have been so scared."

"Yes, he did. He is a real hero. And the Five witches, too."

We paused. I wanted to cheer her up. But in reality, it seemed like she was trying to cheer me up.

"What was it like flying on a broomstick through the air like that?"

"Well, I couldn't believe what was going on. It all happened in a blink of an eye. We flew so fast. And we could see the whole city from way up in the sky."

"And you could see the city through all that fog?"

"There's no fog up high in the sky. The fog is only right near the ground. And you want to know something else? The Five witches heard everything."

"What do you mean?"

"The Five witches overheard Pashelle talk to Wanda. They heard the whole conversation. And Pashelle didn't say anything to Wanda."

"How do they know this?"

"Because they were there. They were listening. And after Pashelle ran away from Wanda, they heard Panic and Prime talk about how they were going to tell on Pashelle. That they were going to try to get Pashelle into trouble. The Five witches said that if we need them to tell the truth about what really happened, we only have to ask them."

"Well, that's a relief. Isn't it?"

"Yeah. Panic is a goof," said Pavneet, as she let out a really big sneeze.

"I think it's time for you go back to the hospital and rest."

"I'm going to miss out on all the fun tonight, aren't I?"

"Haven't you had enough fun for one night? Were you scared in that house?"

"Oh my God. I'm never ever going into a person's house ever again. That was just brutal. What a crazy old lady she was."

"I know, right. Maybe we should have let Pashelle burn her to death."

"Maybe she is dead. She hit her head really hard. And she didn't even open her eyes after."

"She got knocked out cold."

We started walking slowly back toward the main entrance.

"I should go this way. I have to go and check up on Pannette."

"What do you mean?"

"She's with me at the hospital. Dr. Pumpkin gave her a choice. That she could do her twenty hours of service by spending time with me at the hospital tonight, even though it meant she missed tonight's celebration, or do one hour for three weeks."

"Four weeks."

"No, it's three … Aren't you counting weekends?" she asked.

"Oh. Yeah, okay."

"So Pannette said she would stay by my side. She told me she didn't care about the celebration."

And I finally said to Pavneet what I had wanted to say to her since I got back to the Patch.

"I'm so sorry. I'm so sorry. I'm so sorry." I buried my head in my hands. Pavneet opened my hands. "I knew you were sick and tired and could hardly walk. And we didn't slow down for you at all. We just kept running to the next house, trying to get more candy. It was like I didn't even care about you. Didn't even care about one of my dearest friends in all the world. That was such a mean thing to do, and I am never, ever going to leave you alone like that ever again."

"It's okay, Petrina." As she wiped the tears away from my eyes and held me close, I started to cry again. This time they were tears of shame. It was a roller-coaster of a Halloween night.

"No, it's not okay. And you are being so nice to me right now. I was wrong to leave you behind." My voice was quivering. I could hardly say the words coming out of my mouth. I didn't even care if I composed myself enough to speak properly.

"It's okay. Let it go. I'm safe. We're all safe."

I thought to myself that I was lucky to have a friend like Pavneet.

"It's all for the best. Now I can finally leave my house. For good."

"And you are moving in with me. You will be my roommate."

"And Peter's, too."

"For sure."

After another long pause, she said, "Geez, Petrina … You cried just as much as Pannette did."

We both smiled.

"I'm going. I will talk to you tomorrow. We can eat all the candy we want." She tried to change the subject to cheer me up. Imagine that. And yes, we could. The day after Halloween was the only day of the year we could eat as much candy and chocolate as we wanted. After that, candy was given out in even portions as dessert, each day, until it was finished. She said bye as I gave her another hug. I wiped the tears from my eyes and tried to compose myself as I reentered the center.

CHAPTER 13
GRADUATION

By this time, the lobby had cleared. It was empty. Everyone must have gone to the arena for the closing ceremony. I walked eastward toward the lounge. Just before reaching the lounge, I went out the doors on the right, walked a short distance on a path through the Carnation Garden, and entered the arena. It was crowded. Most of the pumpkins were standing just inside the walls, as it only seats around five hundred pumpkins. The arena was beautifully decorated. I know because I helped decorate it.

I tried to locate Peter, but there were too many faces to search, and I gave up. Many pumpkins had gone out as ghosts. I stood near the door. I listened instead to Ms. Pumpkin give her Closing Ceremony speech. A speech that would normally be given by Pudge. Again, I'm not going to recite the whole speech to you; I'm sure you can find a copy of this one online as well. It was a nice speech. She was explaining how pumpkins go through a maturation process of learning and soaking up everything in life. She talked about the new responsibilities that the graduating pumpkins would now have. How they would now volunteer their lives for the good of the Patch. And how they have to set a good example for the rest of us. And how they must accept these responsibilities as adults.

"How come you're all wet? Your eyes are all red." Plato had seen me come in and had gotten out of his seat and now stood next to me. "Do you want to sit down?"

"No, Plato. Thanks, but I'm fine." He's so polite.

Pashelle and Polo soon joined us.

"How come you're all wet?" Pashelle asked.

"I was talking to Pavneet outside. She told me everything that Peter did."

"The Five witches helped Peter find Pavneet," she said.

"Why did they help?" I asked her, still trying to wipe the rain, and tears, from my eyes.

"Do you remember when Peter helped one of them when she fell down off her broom? Well, they wanted to help Peter in the same way he had helped her. And they can prove that I didn't tell Wanda anything about the candy, and …"

"I know. Pavneet told me."

"Panic admitted that everything he said was a lie. So now I am free. Finally. But only Panic. Panic also admitted that it was his idea and that Prime didn't have anything to do with it. But I think Prime is still in trouble for not coming out and saying something. Actually, the Five witches overheard everything. Do you know what happened …"

"I know. I know what happened, Pashelle."

"Did you know that Prime told all of this to Peter?"

"Really?"

She nodded and started again. "And some of the elders think that Pavneet was sick all along. They can't prove it, but they suspected something was wrong. They gave her a lecture about being honest. That if she had told them she was sick, they could have provided extra blankets and given her proper medicine to make her feel better, and ..."

"They knew she was sick."

"Really?" she said, after a brief pause.

"I'll tell you later. Or Pavneet can tell you. She probably got worse. Spending all that time outside in the cold. And who knows what infection she got after being snatched up by those witches."

We stopped talking so we could listen to Ms. Pumpkin on the stage. But only for a minute or so. "So in conclusion ..."

Pashelle turned to me again, and I saw a tear come out of her eye. "We were bad pumpkins today, Petrina. I want to go to the hospital and talk to Pavneet, but I don't know what to say to her, to even begin explaining what terrible ..."

I didn't want to cry again, so I tried changing the subject quickly. "Do you think we should tell someone we went into that house?" I asked her.

"No. No way. That's enough trouble for one day, don't you think?"

"I guess so. We'll leave it. We'll just say that, with all the commotion that went on, we forgot to mention it."

We were so bad, I know.

"What will happen to Panic?" I asked.

"I don't know. But he's not here. He was just taken to the office. I wouldn't be surprised if he had to spend the night there and missed the party tonight."

"I hope he gets in big trouble."

Just then, Ms. Pumpkin, who was standing near the door with us, stared at us angrily, imploring us to be quiet, and to pay attention to the ceremony. We decided that would be best.

Ms. Pumpkin was now giving instructions to the seniors, who were all seated separately near the side of the stage.

One by one, the names of the graduating pumpkins were called. In alphabetical order, of course. The first to walk across the stage and get his diploma was Patti Pumpkin. Patti is indeed male, although it sounds like he has a female name. He walked across the stage, shook hands with about seven Elected Elders who were also on the stage, accepted his diploma, said "Thank you" to all of us, and stood near the far wall on the stage. And in return, in a big, loud collective voice, the whole arena replied, "Thank you, Mr. Pumpkin!"

I don't think I have ever spoken with Patti. But as you know, I will never refer to him as Patti. It will be "Mr. Pumpkin" from now on. That is another perk of graduating. After I graduate, all little pumpkins will call me Ms. Pumpkin. Imagine that. Peers are allowed to call you by your real name. So one day when I graduate, and if I ever meet Patti, I will call him Patti. One day it will be okay for me to say Papi again. That put a smile on my face.

You might think this is kind of weird, calling every elder "Mr." or "Ms." But to us, this is a sign of respect to elders. When you graduate, you achieve something special. Well, anyway, it was like what Ms. Pumpkin said in her speech.

One by one, the graduating pumpkins marched across the stage, received their diplomas, shook hands, and made a small speech. We greeted each one with a loud and cheery "Thank you, Mr. or Ms. Pumpkin."

As the last of the seniors walked across the stage to receive the diploma, and the closing ceremony was ending, I tried searching for Peter again, but there was still no sign of him. I waited near the door, hoping to find him as everyone exited the arena. There were too many to track, however, and some left from the two other doors on the other side.

Pumpkins were now setting up the arena with beds. Anyone who wanted to sleep here in the Eye, could sleep here. If there was going to be any sleep at all. After the experience we had all gone through, who was actually going to sleep tonight? Not me, that's for sure. Tonight was going to be a giant slumber party. Pashelle and Polo formed in the line to talk to Ms. Pumpkin regarding our sleeping arrangements. And Plato left my side to meet with Priscilla and Petunia. It seemed more and more that Plato appreciated talking to older pumpkins. I think he found the conversation more stimulating. Priscilla and Petunia would be seniors the following year.

After the ceremony, when all the pumpkins split up into smaller groups and were scattered all over the center and the arena, I finally saw Peter in the kitchen. I wanted to say hello to him, but I couldn't get the chance. He was talking to Mr. Pumpkin, Pavol, and Parker. I followed Peter around the Eye, waiting for my chance to say hello and greet him, but every time I got near him, someone else started talking to him. Porter was telling him how his evening went with the communal group.

I wasn't able to sit next to him during dinner, either. He was with Porter, Peanut, Penny, and a few other pumpkins that I didn't even recognize. And by the time Pudge cut the closing ceremony cake, I lost track of him again. But then I would find him again ... but with someone else. For hours into the night, he was never alone. It would seem that everyone was probably thanking him for what he had done that evening, but that wasn't necessarily true, either. When I did get up close to him, I stood next to him and listened to his conversations. No one really dwelled on his heroic evening. Instead, they were talking about other things, things that they had done together before Halloween and things they were going to do in the coming days, after Halloween. He was constantly surrounded by pumpkins no matter where he went. Pumpkins whom I had never met before.

"Hey, Petrina, what a night! What a glorious night! Have you spoken with Peter yet?"

"No. Not yet." It was Palmer. What did he want?

"Oh. I was with Peter and Parker and some of the elders earlier. And they were talking about the storage of the candy. I think I know where it is … I think that …"

I lost track of Peter again. I was distracted by the pumpkin band, which was carrying its equipment into the arena. I thought Paris might sing.

"Not now, Palmer, okay?" I didn't realize Palmer was Peter's friend. I followed the pumpkin band into the arena. I asked Palmer about his friendship with Peter.

"Peter and I hang out all the time. He comes over to my place, and sometimes I come over to yours. I really like that painting of the stars and the sky hanging over your bed. That's so cool."

Palmer had been to my house and seen my painting? Strange that I had never noticed Palmer and Peter together. I normally pay such great attention to detail.

Throughout the night, pumpkins were coming up to me and telling me how Peter was such a good pumpkin and how they valued his thoughtfulness, kindness, and friendship. Everyone seemed to have known Peter, even before the heroics. Everyone had a story to tell.

Prudence Pumpkin was telling me how one day, not long ago, some older pumpkins were bothering her, and Peter stood up to them. He told them to get lost, in a very sharp, stern voice. And those pumpkins, not wanting to cause a scene, actually left Prudence alone.

Patience Pumpkin came up to me and said she and Peter had done lots of things together over the past year. That they often discussed ideas and projects—things that we could do to make the Patch a better and safer place to live. They recently worked on a project about building an indoor swimming pool, so that we could all learn how to swim and not be so afraid of the water. They had submitted this project to the Elected Elders.

How did he know all these pumpkins? How did all these pumpkins know him?

And it suddenly dawned on me. Something I had never realized before, after following him around for hours. Peter was not a loner. And all this time, I had thought he was. He was cheerful and happy and seemed very comfortable in this crowd, talking and laughing with everyone. Peter was not quiet. He spoke his mind and was loud and clear when he talked. Peter was not afraid. He was courageous enough to save Pavneet like he did. He was smart enough to get information from Prime and provide a favor for the Five witches so that they would return the favor.

Peter is kind and gentle and funny and thoughtful. I watched him circulate around the Eye, and he was enjoying himself, having a blast. I found myself right near the dance floor of the arena, still trying to get his attention. And for a minute, I thought I had my chance, but then the pumpkin band started playing, and he was invited onto the dance floor. He started dancing and singing. Then he fell down. Aw. But he seemed okay. He got back up. Peanut helped him get up from the ground. He must have slipped on some water or something. He didn't seem to care, though, since, when he got back up off the floor, he started dancing again. And laughing. And smiling. And I was smiling with him. And for the tenth time this evening, tears spilled from my eyes.

For the first time in my life, I felt a connection with Peter. For the first time in my life, I wanted to talk to him, and hold him. For the first time in my life, I felt proud to say that Peter was my brother. I had been wrong about him all this time. He does have friends.

Peter Pumpkin has lots of friends.

Printed in the United States
By Bookmasters

To Cindy,

Peter Nanra